A Cowboy's Seduction

DIAMOND LAKES, TEXAS

CYNTHIA D'ALBA

Riante Romance

Praise for Cynthia D'Alba

"Outstanding love story."

—Avid Reader, Amazon on *A Cowboy's Seduction*

"This book was fun and I loved every page of it."

—Connie, Goodreads on *A Cowboy's Seduction*

"This author does an amazing job of keeping readers on their toes while maintaining a natural flow to the story."

—RT Book Reviews on *Texas Hustle*

"Cynthia D'Alba's *Texas Fandango* from Samhain lets readers enjoy the sensual fun in the sun [...] This latest offering gives readers a sexy escape and a reason to seek out D'Alba's earlier titles."

—Library Journal Reviews on *Texas Fandango*

"[...] inclusions that stand out for all the right reasons is Cynthia D'Alba's clever *Backstage Pass*"

—Publisher's Weekly on *Backstage Pass* in *Cowboy Heat*

"*Texas Two Step* kept me on an emotional roller coaster [...] *Texas Two Step* is an emotionally charged romance, with well-developed characters and an engaging secondary cast. A quarter of the way into the book I added Ms. D'Alba to my auto-buys."

—5 Stars and Recommended Read, Guilty Pleasure Book Reviews on *Texas Two Step*

"I loved this book. The characters came alive. They had depth, interest and completeness. But more than the romance and sex which were great, there are connections with family and friends which makes this story so much more than a story about two people."

—Night Owl Romance 5 STARS! A TOP PICK on *Texas Bossa Nova*

"Wow, what an amazing romance novel. *Texas Lullaby* is an impassioned, well-written book with a genuine love story that took hold of my heart and soul from the very beginning."

—LJT, Amazon Reviews, on *Texas Lullaby*

"An emotional, complex and beautiful story of love and life and how it can all change in a heartbeat."

—DiDi, Guilty Pleasures Book Reviews on *Texas Lullaby*

"*TEXAS LULLABY* is a refreshing departure from the traditional romance plot in that it features an already committed couple."

—Tangled Hearts Book Reviews on *Texas Lullaby*

"A great read with just the right amount of steamy sexual tension and a HEA!"

—D. Yochum, Just The Write Touch, on Cadillac Cowboy

A Cowboy's Seduction

By Cynthia D'Alba

Cover Artist: Valerie Tibbs

Editor: Delilah Devlin

For Tina Reiter and Jessica Sheehan of the D'Alba Diamonds. A thousand thank yous for your beta reads and excellent suggestions and edits. And a special thank you to Tina for all your ass-kicking and pushing me while I wrote this.
There are no better critique partners in the world than Sandi Jones and Angela Campbell. Thank you for helping me keep my deadline.

One

Natalie Diamond's eardrums throbbed in rhythm to the slap of her windshield wipers that struggled to keep the falling sleet from coating her car's glass. She flipped the radio off; she couldn't hear it over the ice pings and chattering wiper blades anyway. Plus, with all the crazy Memphis drivers who loved to whip in and out of traffic as though it were a beautiful spring day instead of a dreary, icy December evening, she needed the quiet to concentrate. When she and Tim had divorced, he'd kept the house in Southern California and she'd moved back to her childhood home in Memphis. She'd been mentally prepared for the sweltering summer heat, but this unusual ice storm so close to Christmas hadn't been on her radar.

Through the fogged-up windshield, the red taillights of the car in front of her comprised the vast majority of her total visibility. Shoving her left hand into the pocket on the driver's door, she blindly searched for something to wipe off the windshield haze. Her fingers snagged a used napkin from her last drive-through meal. Leaning forward, she wiped at the glass over the steering wheel. Bright red opaque smears replaced the hazy fog.

Great. Now the windshield looked like the set for Texas Chainsaw Massacre III—or were they up to four or five by now?

Natalie dropped the used napkin with the open ketchup packet to the floor between her feet and began trying to remove the crimson blotches with her gloved hand. All that accomplished was spreading the smudges further on the glass while staining her best pair of gloves.

Super. Between the crappy weather and her demanding boss, this really had been the day from hell. The only thing keeping her from jumping from the Memphis Bridge into the Mississippi was the upcoming two weeks of vacation with her parents in Florida, ideally every day a sun-filled roast at the beach.

By the time she turned on Cherry Lane, tension tied stone-hard knots in her shoulders and neck. She slid to a stop at the mailbox and lowered her window just enough to shove her arm out. Tiny shards of ice jumped down her sleeve. She hurriedly pulled out green and red envelopes, stuffed, she was sure, with jolly holiday greetings.

After parking, she dragged plastic market bags from the passenger seat floorboard onto the front seat, dropped the mail and her purse into one of the sacks, and then slipped the sacks over her wrist like a collection of bracelets. She made a mad dash for the door. Jumping icy puddles and an accumulation of muck on the sidewalk, she leapt up the stairs to get under the porch roof.

She shook her head. Water slung off the tip of her blonde ponytail. The grocery bags slithered off her arms onto the wooden porch as she dug the keys from her front pants pocket. After unlocking the door, she propped it open, pushed the groceries through with her foot, and kicked it shut.

Leaving her wet shoes and ruined gloves on the entrance rug, she ambled through the living room toward the kitchen for a much needed two-fingers of bourbon, scanning the return addresses on the envelopes as she walked. Lots of Christmas cards. A few bills. Nothing that couldn't wait.

She poured two fingers of Maker's Mark, studied the level, and then poured a little more. She toasted having survived the day and lifted the thin rim of the glass to her lips.

Her house phone rang just as the first delicious dram of whiskey slid down her throat. She leaned over and snatched up the receiver.

"Hello?"

"Hi, honey. It's Mom."

Natalie pulled out a chair at her kitchen table, sat, and settled in for a long chat, which was typical for talks with Sissy Diamond. Phone calls from her mother were never short. "Hi, Mom. How's the weather down there?"

3

"Beautiful. Close to eighty today. I don't know why your father and I waited so long to move." She sighed. "Should have done this ten years ago."

Natalie chuckled. "Yes, I know. You tell me that every time you call. I'm looking forward to soaking up some of your sun next week."

"Oh, honey. That's why I called. You remember the Duncans, right? Lee and Joey? Well, they were scheduled to go on a holiday Mediterranean cruise with the Freemans next door. Well, poor Lee had a heart attack last night and now they can't go and the Freemans asked if we wanted to go on the cruise in Joey and Lee's place. Isn't that marvelous? Not Lee's heart attack, of course, but you know I've always wanted to see Greece, which is one of the stops, so your father and I just had to say yes. I told your father that you would understand."

"So, you're going to be gone Christmas and New Year's?" Natalie's heart sank. No Florida. No sun. No heat to melt her frozen toes.

"Yes. Isn't it thrilling? I know you were coming down, but with all the friends you have in Memphis, I told your father you'd never miss us."

Her mother's voice was giddy with excitement. What could Natalie say? She wouldn't throw a wet blanket on her mother's joy. She glanced outside. Maybe an *ice* blanket would be a better analogy.

"You definitely have to go, Mom. You can't miss this chance. What's Dad saying about going?"

"Oh, you know your father. He'd sit in his recliner and watch sports all day if I let him."

Natalie chuckled. "Yeah, I know Dad. When do you leave?"

"Three days! I've got so much to do before then. I don't have any clothes that'll work for a cruise."

Her mother's closet rods groaned from the weight of all her clothes. Natalie suspected her mother had an appropriate wardrobe for any occasion, but then, shopping was one of her mother's favorite activities.

"Sounds like fun, Mom. Wish I could be there to shop with you."

"Me, too. I'd better run. I dropped your Christmas present in the mail to you this morning. You should have it tomorrow. I think you'll enjoy it."

"Oh. Thanks." Natalie glanced toward the wrapped presents for her parents. "Your gifts are here. I was bringing them with me. I could mail them to you, I guess."

"Don't bother. We'll come up next month and take you out to dinner. You'll need the break from taxes, I'm sure."

"Sure, sure. Well, have fun. Tell Dad hi for me."

Natalie hung up the phone and blew out a long, frustrated breath. Damn. She was stuck in Memphis for Christmas. Even if her mother had offered Natalie their Florida condo while they were gone, she wouldn't have accepted. She knew no one down there, other than her parents and a few of their friends.

When she and Tim had been married and living in California, Christmas had been an ongoing series of parties, moving from one couple's house to another's. They hadn't had a slow evening starting a couple of weeks before Christmas and running through New Year's Eve.

When he'd left her for another woman, he'd kept all their friends. too. That had hurt her...a lot. But now, she had a wonderful set of friends here in Memphis who would be happy to host her for the holidays. That wasn't her problem. Her problem was Natalie craved sun and warmth, not cold and dreary.

Sleet clicked on her bedroom window glass like long fingernails. Natalie snuggled deeper into her flannel sheets and tucked the heavy blanket under her chin. As she was dropping back into the dream about the stacks of tax returns on her desk that were overdue, her eyes flew open and searched for the clock. Good lord. Eight-thirty. She was late for work.

But even as the thought passed through her brain, she remembered she was on vacation until after the first of the year. With a smile, she settled back into the warm covers and closed her eyes. She had an entire month away from the office before all hell broke loose in January with tax returns. She enjoyed being an accountant, even if she didn't particularly like where she worked, or her boss. She loved numbers. They made sense and always added up.

Unlike, say, her love life.

But damn. Even she realized that being an

accountant was boring. What was that old joke? What does an accountant use for birth control? Her personality. Yep. That was her. Smart but dull. Predictable and staid.

She was drifting off, dreaming of some mysterious man who would sweep her away from her crazy boss and spice up her predictable life when her doorbell rang. Rolling over, she decided to ignore it.

Bing Bong! Then, knock, knock, knock.

She pulled the pillow over her head.

Bing-bong! Pound, pound, pound.

"Fine," she muttered, tossing the covers back. "I'm up."

After a fast stop for a heavy robe and fluffy slippers, she shuffled to the door.

"Good morning," a young man dressed in a FedEx uniform said, his words coming out in a frosty fog. "I have a delivery that requires a signature."

Frigid air rushed in to replace the warmth, and she shivered. After she signed the electronic signature pad, he handed her a priority envelope. "Have a good day."

She locked the door and looked at the return address. Her parents. Right. Her mother had said she was sending a Christmas present. Whatever it was could wait until she got her coffee going. Knowing her mother, it was undoubtedly a sizable gift card to some department store. Sissy Diamond was always trying to spruce up Natalie's wardrobe.

Her house shoes slapped against the wood flooring as she scuffed into the kitchen. She pulled the coffee beans from the cabinet, ground them, and got the coffee dripping. She sat down at the kitchen table and ripped open the FedEx envelope. A letter in her mother's handwriting slipped out.

Dear Natalie– Your father and I know how much you were looking forward to getting out of Memphis and down to Florida for some beach time. Even though our plans have changed this year, we didn't want you to miss out on the sun. I know how you love your tans.

Not exactly. It was her mother who loved to tan. Natalie loved to stay under the umbrella with a book.

Surprise! We are sending you on an all-expense-paid vacation to the Sand Castle Resort in the Caribbean. You fly out of Memphis on December fourteenth and return on December twenty-fourth. That gives you two days to go buy some island-appropriate clothes. I've enclosed a VISA gift card with six hundred dollars on it.

Well, she'd been partially right. There was a gift card and shopping involved.

Your airline and hotel confirmations are in the envelope with this letter, in case you haven't found them yet.

Natalie shook two pages of confirmations out of the FedEx envelope, along with a VISA gift card in a presentation folder.

Have fun. We'll miss you. We'll see you in January, and you can tell us all about it.

Love you,

Mom and Dad

P.S. You'll need your passport so make sure it's up to date.

Natalie fell heavily against the back of her chair in shock. Her gut whirled from the surprise. Her heart pounded loudly in her ears. This was an incredible gift. It was as if her parents had heard her whining last night about her need to get out of Memphis for the holidays and had sprung into action. They had always been generous with her, but this...? Well, this was more than generous. A completely paid-for vacation. But man, she hated shopping like some people hated taxes, but—she worked the VISA card between her fingers like a card magician—her mother had been correct. She had nothing in her closet for a Caribbean vacation.

She sucked down her coffee then headed to her room to dress. Crummy weather or not, she was going shopping. Heaven help her.

Two

B rock Wade zipped his fly then headed for the kitchen to slug down his usual cup of coffee and toast before heading out to the barn. The aroma of freshly-baked biscuits and bacon met him at the top of the stairs, causing him to pause. Something was up. Usually, he was the only person awake at this hour. Plus, his breakfast was normally a cup of coffee and a microwaved frozen sausage and biscuit.

Yeah, one of his siblings had done something, broke something, or wrecked something and needed him to fix, replace, or apologize. With a long-suffering sigh, he walked down the stairs and turned into the kitchen.

As he suspected, his three younger siblings were seated around the table...a table laden with scrambled eggs, biscuits, and crisp sausage. He eyed them with suspicion as he pulled down a mug from the cabinet and filled it with strong coffee.

Leaning his hip against the counter, he took a

large swallow of coffee to brace himself for whatever these three were up to. He took another gulp of his caffeine of choice and said, "Not that I'm not happy to see all of you this morning; however, the last time the three of you got up at the crack of dawn to gang up on me, it was to convince me to let Lauren stay out until 2 a.m. for the homecoming dance."

A flush crept up Lauren's neck, as well it should. Brock had had to pick her up from a post-homecoming party after her date had become too drunk to drive.

"And that turned out so well," Brock said with a hike of his eyebrow.

George snorted, then tried to cover it by bringing his cup to his mouth. At twenty-two, George still found a lot of humor in drunks. Brock had been too busy and overwhelmed at twenty-two to find humor in much of anything.

"So, does someone want to tell me why we are having a family meeting at—" Brock looked at the clock on the stove, "—five-thirty-five in the morning?"

"We will," Cody said. "We're waiting on—"

The kitchen door opened with a bang against the wall as a gust of frigid Texas December air shot in, depositing a dusting of snow on the linoleum. Hank Brown, the ranch foreman, stomped into the house.

"Whew," he said, brushing ice off his felt cowboy hat. "Nasty out there."

Brock frowned. "What are you doing here, Hank?"

Hank looked at the three Wade siblings, who stared back at him.

Brock pulled out a chair, sat, and then filled a plate with bacon, scrambled eggs, and hot biscuits. "I don't have time for games this morning. It's crappy outside, and I've got a lot to do. So..." He shoved a biscuit loaded with butter and bacon into his mouth and chewed. "Either start talking or I'm gone as soon as I finish eating."

Hank poured himself a cup of coffee, then turned a chair around and straddled it.

Lauren pulled a paper gift sack from under her chair and set it on the table. "Merry Christmas!" A wide smile lit her face. The twinkle in her eyes had all his mental alarms beeping.

Brock took a swig of his coffee and eyed the Christmas sack, now more than a little suspicious about what his siblings were up to.

"It ain't Christmas," he growled. "And you know the rule...no unwrapping presents before December twenty-fifth, and, unless I'm mistaken, that's still a couple of weeks away."

"But, Brock, this one can't wait until then." Lauren, the youngest and most vocal of the Wade clan, pushed the bag toward him. "Please. Just look inside." Not only was she the youngest and most vocal, but also the sibling who had him wrapped around her little finger.

When Brock didn't immediately reach for the Santa sack, Cody elbowed him. "Pick up the sack. We all know your rules but, for today, be flexible."

Brock shrugged. "I'm flexible," he muttered, glaring at Cody, and then spreading his glare across the rest of the family.

George laughed. "Yeah, about as flexible as a fence post, and you know what happens to those when they fight the wind from a tornado like Lauren."

Reaching across the table, Brock tugged the sack toward him. He reached inside and pulled out a piece of notebook paper.

For all you've done for us and all you do for us, we are sending you on a ten-day vacation to the Sand Castle Resort.

Merry Christmas

Cody, George, and Lauren

Accompanying the letter were printed confirmations for a hotel and flight reservations. The flight was scheduled for the day after tomorrow.

He furrowed his brow. "What's this?"

His sister jumped up, ran around the table, and threw her arms around his neck. "A vacation. Just for you. From us."

"Thanks, honey, but I don't have time to go on a vacation. There's too much work that still has to be done to get the cattle moved up closer to the house, not to mention all the Christmas shopping and decorating that hasn't been started. I appreciate the thought. I really do. Maybe next year, but not now. Not this year."

"You have to go now." Lauren insisted. "It's all paid for and everything." Her bottom lip poked out in a pout as a frown pulled down her eyebrows.

Brock turned and wrapped his arms around his baby sister. "It's so sweet you wanted to do this." He looked at his brothers. "You guys, too. But now just isn't a good time."

"Why not?" Cody challenged. "You think we can't do without you for ten lousy days?"

"It's not that," Brock protested. "It's—"

"What? Hell, Brock. Me and George can run this ranch for a couple of weeks."

"I know that, Cody. But—"

Cody stood. "I'm twenty-nine. I've been working with you at Ace in the Hole all my life, and you still don't trust me."

"I trust you. It's just that—"

George shoved his chair back with a loud scrape. "Is it me that you don't trust? When you were my age, you'd been raising us all by yourself for three years. What do you have that I don't? What's it gonna take before you let Cody and me shoulder some of the ranch's responsibilities?"

His three siblings stood, forming a united front. Anger on Cody's face. Frustration etched on George's expression. And Lauren looked about one second away from a flood of tears. Brock let out a long sigh.

Damn it. He didn't need a vacation. He didn't want a vacation. And he certainly didn't want to go to some resort he'd never heard of on a Caribbean island he'd never heard of.

"Fine," he finally said. "I'll think about it. We can talk about it tonight at dinner."

Lauren flipped her long, dark hair over one shoulder. "There's nothing to talk about. Either you accept our present, or I'll never speak to you again." She wheeled around and stomped out of the kitchen.

Brock rubbed at a headache he hadn't had ten minutes ago. Addressing his brothers, he asked, "So, can I expect that both of you will refuse to talk to me, too?"

"Hell, no," Cody said. "But you can expect we might beat the crap out of your ungrateful ass. Lauren has been working on this surprise for at least six months. Doing research on various resorts. Checking flights. Reading reviews. Think about that all day. Then come home and pack your damn bags for a vacation that you will go on and you will enjoy."

George crossed his arms. "Ditto."

Brock studied Cody. When had his little brother become his own man? And when had George grown up?

"We'll talk about it tonight," Brock bit out.

Cody threw on his heavy coat, a pair of thick gloves and headed out the kitchen door with George right on his boot heels.

As the Wade family drama had played out, Hank Brown had watched, drank three cups of coffee and added nothing to the conversation.

Brock refilled his mug and sat again. "You knew about this." It wasn't a question as much as an accusation.

Hank nodded, not cowed at all by Brock being his boss. After all, Hank and his wife had been a part

16

of Ace in the Hole Ranch since before George was born.

"And yet you did nothing to stop this ridiculous idea?"

Hank crossed his arms on the table and leaned on them. "Nothing ridiculous about it. They're right. You need a vacation."

"Bullshit. I need to be here to make sure the ranch doesn't fail. I have to make sure they have a home. I have bills to pay. Obligations. You know that."

"What I know is that fourteen years ago your parents died, and you had to grow up really fast. I know that you haven't left your brothers or sister for even a day since then. I know that you gave up college, a dating life, and all of your twenties to make sure those kids had clothes, food, and a roof over their heads. You haven't had a girlfriend in so long that Lauren actually wondered if you were gay."

"She did not," Brock said with a chuckle, but that quickly faded when Hank didn't laugh along.

"Yeah, she did. Course I told her she watched too much television, but then I realized that she probably hadn't ever seen you go on what you call dates and what I call bar hook-ups."

Brock flinched. "Doesn't matter. I'll get away one day. Lauren will graduate from high school this year, and then—"

"And then you'll find some other reason why you can't leave." Hank reached out and squeezed Brock's shoulder. "The Missus and I talked about this, and

17

we agree with the kids. Cody is old enough to have more responsibilities around here than you give him. George, too. Lauren is maturing so fast now that it won't be long before she'll be wanting to be more involved. You have to let them grow up. You can't keep doing everything for them."

Brock scraped his fingers through his hair. "I don't know, Hank. A vacation? In the Caribbean?"

Hank laughed. "You make it sound like you're being sent to Alcatraz." He grew serious. "You'll break their hearts if you don't go. They want to do something for you. Look at it this way, they're telling you how much they appreciate all you've done to keep this family together. Don't take that away from them."

Hank stood and slapped his hat back on. "It's your decision, of course. But I have to warn you...I might have to join the boys in kicking your ass if you don't go." He slipped his thick coat back on. "I'll see you at the barn."

When Brock finally had the kitchen to himself, he pulled the papers back out. A vacation. Damnedest thing. Other than a regional rodeo or stock sale, he had never been on anything like a vacation.

He shook his head. Wearing shorts in December. Didn't seem natural to him.

Well, damn. It wasn't as if he had any choice. He was going on a vacation he didn't want to a place he'd never heard of whether he wanted to go or not.

Three

Two days later, Natalie found a seat at gate C1 at Memphis International Airport, a coffee in one hand and her digital reader in the other. However, as a diehard people-watcher, it was almost impossible to read when there were so many fascinating people in the area. such as the knockout blonde dressed in a pair of painted-on white shorts and Christmas shirt with reindeer buttons straining to stay in their holes. Natalie covertly studied the... um... colorful shirt. It was either filled with store-bought breasts or the woman was smuggling a couple of bowling balls. That must've been some strong thread holding those buttons on.

The woman's blonde hair lay in waves along her shoulder blades. Her face...well, her face could have been on the cover of Cosmopolitan or Elle. Beautiful. Tan. Make-up perfect. Eyelashes dark and curled. Lips red and full. Natalie decided on the spot she'd never stand next to this woman. Beside her, she'd look like a scrub pine in the middle of a forest of blooming dogwoods.

The could-have-been-a-model woman was sitting next to a short, stubby man with straight black hair tied with a brown leather band at the nape of his neck. He wore blue denim shorts and a yellow polo. His brown sandals looked cushy and comfortable and battered from extensive wear. He wasn't what Natalie would call handsome, but his face had interesting angles and curves. The entire time he was talking with Ms. Blonde-Ample-Breasts, his stare never reached above her collarbone. She didn't seem to notice or care where his gaze landed and laughed at everything he said.

Natalie had just forced her eyes off the odd couple and onto her reader when a pair of scuffed cowboy boots passed within her eyesight. Her gaze walked its way up a pair of faded jeans over muscular thighs to a tight ass. It was only as he walked into the men's restroom that she realized she'd twisted in her seat to keep admiring his backside. The old saying '" Save a horse, ride a cowboy," flashed into her mind. It'd been years since she'd ridden a horse, never mind a cowboy. Wouldn't it be nice to find someone like him at the Sand Castle Resort?

The gate attendant announced boarding for first-class passengers, passengers traveling with small children, and anyone needing a little extra time in boarding. Natalie glanced around the gate area, disappointed she hadn't seen that hunky cowboy again. She could have all the blues and jazz musicians she wanted in Memphis, but a real cowboy? Not so much. Oh well. Such was life. Natalie collected her belongings and boarded with the other first-class passengers.

Traveling on her parents' nickel was nice, to say the least. The only kind of airline ticket her mother knew how to buy was first class, something Natalie would never have sprung for on her own. Being in first class certainly had its pros and cons, however.

Pro...early boarding. Con...other passengers looking at you as they passed.

Pro...alcoholic beverages available before departing. Con...the dadgum other passengers looking longingly at your drink.

But then the biggest pro of all walked onto the plane. Pro...seeing the hunky cowboy from the concourse walking past as he found his seat farther back in the plane. There was no con to that one, except he wasn't sitting next to her.

Of course, him being on the same flight did not mean they were headed to the same final destination since they had a short layover in San Juan. She had to change planes, and she bet many of the other passengers were also catching connecting flights, but a girl could dream.

She lost track of her hunky cowboy in the Puerto Rico airport. The layover between flights was only thirty minutes, just enough time to hit the ladies' room. The flight was loading when she finally found the right gate. She raced onto the plane and dropped into her assigned seat, 1A. The small prop plane was full at twenty passengers, and she didn't expect to know anyone else there. She was wrong.

She did recognize someone. The woman wearing the button-busting Christmas shirt was seated next to her. As soon as the plane was airborne, the woman turned to her.

"Hi. I'm Amanda Cummings. Everybody calls me Mandy." Her voice was light and airy. Her eyes lit with a sparkled with her smiled.

"Natalie Diamond."

"Nice to meet you. Have you been to Sand Castle before?"

Natalie shook her head. "No. Never heard of it until my parents gave me this trip."

"You're going to love it. I noticed you sitting alone at the airport. You meeting someone there?"

Natalie shook her head again.

Mandy laughed quietly. "I am and is he ever going to be surprised."

"He doesn't know you're on the way?"

"Nope. But he'll be thrilled."

"For some reason, I guess I thought you were with the man you were talking to in Memphis."

"Oh, you mean Jeff? Nah. Just someone to chat with while I waited."

"So, tell me more about the resort. I'd love some ideas for what I should do or see while I'm there."

For the remainder of the thirty-minute flight, Mandy clued Natalie in on the best places at the resort to find the hottest guys, the best mixed drinks, and the freshest salads. It was, Mandy assured her, the perfect place to find romance.

While Natalie nodded in the appropriate places, her plan was to soak up some rays, get some badly needed rest, and go home ready for the tax season. Now was not the right time to start a new romance.

Now might not be the right time for a relationship, but it was the right time to leave rigid, boring accountant Natalie in Memphis and let the fun, anything-goes Natalie come out to play.

She wouldn't know a soul at the resort, and she'd bet a million bucks she'd never see any of these people again. *Go and have fun*, she told herself. Flirt. Drink. And if she saw a good-looking guy who really hit her hot button, then she'd let her libido lead the way.

Even as she had the thought, the memory of that tight-assed cowboy crossed her mind. Now, that was what she was talking about. Too bad she hadn't seen him board this plane.

Yep. She was letting Fun Natalie out to play. Heaven knew she hadn't seen hide nor hair of Fun Natalie since college.

The plane landed with a smooth bump. Natalie followed Mandy down the stairs, since the woman appeared to be familiar with the routine. After collecting her checked bag from the plane's belly, she hopped into the back seat of an electric car that'd been built to look like a stretch Hummer. The car could carry six passengers, including the driver.

From his sun-kissed blond hair and vibrant jade-green eyes to his toned tanned body, their driver had heartbreaker written all over him. His khaki shorts rode tight across thighs thick with muscle. His green polo shirt, embroidered with Sand Castle Resort and an illustration of a castle, was snug enough to hint at the six-pack Natalie was sure was beneath. Pinned on the right shoulder was a nametag announcing he was "Thomas."

Natalie would have bet her retirement account that Thomas had a black book of women's names and phone numbers as thick as his flexing biceps.

"Welcome to the Sand Castle Resort," Thomas said, his bright-white smile lighting up his face. "I see some familiar faces and some new ones." He winked at a couple of girls in their early twenties. "Don't hesitate to find me if you have any questions or need something while you're here."

The girls giggled and nudged each other. Natalie chuckled, thinking of all the needs those two might have for Thomas.

As they headed out on a sand and shell path, the harsh sun's rays were filtered through the swaying leaves of mature palm trees. Light dappled the thick growth on either side of the car. Natalie surreptitiously studied the other guests in her car and was disappointed when she realized most of them were female. There was one guy on their tram, but he was snuggled up to the woman beside him. Everything about them screamed *honeymooners*.

Natalie settled back to enjoy the breathtaking scenery. After a ten-minute ride, the cart pulled to a stop in front of a plaza that showcased a large, three-tiered water fountain. Around the edges of the fountain were a variety of blooming flowers and green ferns that swayed in the salty ocean breeze. Across the plaza stood the Sand Castle Resort. Buff-colored, with towers and a rounded roof, the building left the impression it had risen from the sand on which it sat. To enter the castle, visitors had to walk across a drawbridge.

When Natalie turned to exit the car, Thomas was there, holding out his hand to assist her. She smiled and let him help her exit gracefully.

"Impressive," she said, barely able to take her eyes off the building, which was saying something considering her hunky company.

"That it is," he agreed. "I don't believe you've visited the Sand Castle before, have you?"

She turned back to him and tilted her head. "It is my first time. Do I have that much of a rube look?"

He chuckled. "No, but I never forget a beautiful woman. I would remember you."

Flattered, but not buying the line she was sure had been used more than once, she glanced at the castle and back to him. "Have you been here long?"

He shrugged. "About seven years. The resort was still new when I started." His bright-white smile was blinding as he added, "I'll be happy to show you around or answer any questions."

Noticing that the other passengers were headed through the door into the lobby, and she was the last passenger still standing, she returned his smile.

"Thanks for the offer. You never know when I might have a, um, question that needs attention."

He laughed and handed her a card with his phone number. "Call me if I can do anything for you."

"Thanks." She slipped the card into her pocket and headed toward the building she was dying to explore. She strolled through the plaza, stopping for a moment to admire the incredible fountain and flora before starting across the bridge. True to its origin, the drawbridge spanned the castle moat. However, this castle needed no protection.

The moat was a rippling whirl of water pushing laughing couples on inflatable rafts around the corner and out of sight. Other guests floated on their backs or swam along with the rushing waves. How clever to have made a moat part of the resort's water activities.

Stepping inside, she flashed her gaze around, wanting to look everywhere at once. There was so much to take in. A sweeping grand staircase leading to an open mezzanine dominated the lobby. Its brass and tropical woods gleamed under the lighting. A convenience store was tucked under one side of the staircase and, from what she could observe from the hall, was stocked with the usual forgotten items such as toothpaste, magazines, suntan supplies, and a display of condoms that didn't even begin to look subtle.

There was a line at the registration desk. Since she had to wait anyway, she wandered over to the clothing store, aptly named Sand and Surf. Inside were racks of brightly colored tropical shirts, shorts, bikinis, flip-flops, and any other attire one might need while visiting.

A florescent orange bikini drew her. She lifted it from the rack.

"Lovely, isn't it? We just got that in this morning."

Natalie turned toward the husky, sexy female voice. A beautiful woman with shoulder-length blonde hair greeted her from across the store. Even from this distance, Natalie could see the clerk's vivid blue eyes. She wore a white sleeveless blouse with the Sand Castle Resort embroidered across her left breast. The shirt was tied at her waist, where a pink and orange sarong circled a cut-in waist and wrapped around slender hips. On her feet, she wore matching sandals.

"It is. Very." Natalie moved to the floor-length mirror and held up the suit.

"It would look wonderful with your coloring. Is that your size? I'm afraid it's the only one like that we have."

Natalie checked the size. It was perfect. At any store at home, the price would have made her gasp. Considering the shop's locale, the price seemed within reason.

"My size." She smiled at the woman in the mirror. "I think I have to have this."

The woman nodded. "Excellent." She turned to head toward the counter and stopped. Snapping her fingers, she said, "I've got the perfect sarong to go with that. Hold on."

She disappeared behind a curtain. Natalie could hear boxes and paper rattling, and then the woman popped back out. "Here it is," she said, holding up a sarong made of a floral print. The flowers in the design were a perfect color match to the suit. "I remembered ordering this and hoped it might be in today's deliveries. I hadn't even unpacked it."

"I love it," Natalie said. "You knew I'd buy it, didn't you?"

The woman laughed. "How could you not?" She stepped behind the counter to ring up Natalie's purchases. "Do you want to charge this to your room?"

"I haven't even checked in yet," Natalie said with a shake of her head. "This store just kind of sucked me in." She pulled her credit card from her wallet and handed it over. "I'm loving this place. Never seen anything like it."

"Thank you. We work hard to make sure our guests have a good time. Do you know about the bonfire tonight? What am I saying? Of course, you don't. You haven't checked in yet. Tonight, we are having a little welcome party down at the Beachfront Bar. Bonfire. Live music. Dancing. Some light finger foods. Discount drinks. You should come. It'd be a great way to start your vacation."

"Sounds wonderful. I'll make sure I do. What time do all the activities start?"

The woman handed Natalie her purchases in a sack. "Music starts at eight. Usually runs to about eleven or midnight. Kind of depends on the crowd."

"Appreciate it." Natalie started to leave then turned back. "I know there has to be a spa here. I really need a mani-pedi if I want to get this vacation off on the right foot."

"Gotcha. Hold on, and I'll call." She lifted a receiver from under the counter and pushed a couple of buttons. "Manuel. This is Scarlett. I've got..." She paused to look at the charge ticket. "Natalie Diamond checking in today. She really needs a mani-pedi." Scarlett winked. "Let me ask her." She covered the receiver with her palm. "In two hours?"

"Yes. Thank you."

"Right. She'll see you in two hours."

By the time Natalie got back to the lobby to check in, there was only one person in line. As she got into the line, the cowboy from the airport turned from the registration desk. Their gazes met. Natalie's stomach did a little roller coaster loop-the-loop as goosebumps popped up on her arms. He smiled, touched the brim of his hat, and walked out.

"Next."

Natalie jerked her face forward and saw one of the desk clerks waving at her. She hurried over.

"Sorry. I got a little distracted."

"Yes, I saw your distraction." The clerk grinned. "Very nice."

"No kidding." Natalie glanced over her shoulder to see if the cowboy was still in the area, but he was nowhere to be seen. Turning back to the clerk, she said, "I'm Natalie Diamond. I need to check in."

After all the paperwork was done, the clerk laid a

CYNTHIA D'ALBA

resort map on the counter. "We are here," she said, drawing a circle around the castle icon. "Your cabin is number twenty-three. It's here." She circled a small building with the number twenty-three on it. "It's one of our more private cabanas. Very quiet. Very nice. You go through the doors there." She pointed toward a different exit than the one Natalie had used to enter. She turned away, pulled a key off the board behind her, and turned back. "You've been assigned car number ten. Once you get outside, look for a red golf cart that looks like a Corvette. It'll have the number ten on the rear fender."

"Wait. What? A car?"

The clerk smiled. "The only types of transportation on the island are electric golf carts and bikes. Your cabana comes with a cart. I think you'll enjoy it. Your luggage should be already loaded on it. If not, find Joe. He works in that area, and he'll load it for you. Joe, or one of his guys there, will explain how the cart operates. Have a wonderful vacation."

"Thank you," Natalie muttered, still thrown off-guard by the red Corvette car comment. When she got outside, as the clerk had said, her luggage was loaded onto the back end of a small golf cart designed to look like a 1964 Corvette.

Another handsome guy dressed in the Sand Castle Resort uniform hurried up to her. "Ms. Diamond?"

"Yes."

"I'm Joe. I have your car ready to go. Are you familiar with how to charge these?"

30

Actually, she was. Her parents had one in Florida and she'd charged it.

"I am. Where is the charger located?"

"When you get to your cabin, look on the post in the parking area. You'll see the plug-in there. Would you like some help with your luggage?"

She grinned. "Shorts, bikinis, and sundresses don't weigh much. I'll be fine. Thanks."

"Okay, then. Don't hesitate to call if you have any problems. My phone number is on the card clipped to your steering wheel."

She climbed into her "Corvette" and headed off, using the resort map for guidance. Once she left the immediate area around the castle where the parking lots and drives were made of concrete, the roads turned to sand and crushed shell paths like the one she'd been on earlier. She drew in deep breaths of salty air as she flew along the path toward her home for the next ten days. Her shoulders and back began to relax as the tension left her muscles.

The route to her cabana took her past the Beachfront Bar, which was already alive with music and scantily-clad patrons. She wasn't sure what she'd wear tonight, but she felt fairly positive it would be more than a bikini. Regardless of attire, Fun Natalie would definitely be hitting that welcome party.

She passed a number of other individual oceanfront cabanas. She slowed as the cabin numbers reached the twenties, finally turning into the parking space for twenty-three.

For a minute she sat, stunned. She'd expected a

wooden cabin, weathered and small, but boy, had she been wrong.

The bluff exterior of the building was bright with colorful tile inlays. A set of red double doors greeted her. A stone terrace started at the building's entrance and curved around the corner. The sound of waves crashing on shore confirmed what the clerk had told her. Her cabana was very near the ocean's edge.

She slid from the cart and climbed the stairs. After waving her magnetic card in front of the reader, she heard the door lock snick, and she stepped into a room directly from her best fantasy.

Modern, plush furniture in bright floral prints dominated a seating area that overlooked a stone terrace, visible through a wall of glass. Vivid striped recliners and a table with a matching umbrella dominated the rock porch. Just beyond the terrace, the turquoise water of the Caribbean rolled and crashed on the snow-white beach. Sunlight sparkled on the sand granules like a field of tiny diamonds. Fluffy, white clouds floated by in a cerulean blue sky.

Leaving the living room, she made her way to a bedroom, dominated by a massive king-sized bed. Natalie fell onto the bed with a delighted laugh. Her mother had outdone herself this time.

Four

Brock scratched his five o'clock shadow and grinned as he looked around his cabin. When his siblings had gifted this vacation, he'd anticipated a typical hotel setting. But now, he owed his family a major apology for doubting them. Not only was he *not* in a hotel room, his home for the next couple of weeks was an impressive, new cabin within throwing distance of the ocean.

Brightly colored furniture filled the living room but didn't obstruct the view. The bedroom housed a king-sized, four-poster bed facing another wall of glass that showcased the incredible ocean view.

Of course, he'd seen the ocean before, but that had been at Gulf Shores, Alabama. The color of the water in the Gulf of Mexico was no match for the deep blue of the Caribbean. It was like comparing a mule to a thoroughbred racehorse. Both could do the job, but one was a lot prettier.

His life had mostly been comprised of work.

Growing up on a ranch meant he'd learned about hard work from the time he could ride his own horse. But since becoming both mother and father to his siblings when he'd been just eighteen, his life had taken on whole new dimensions, such as trying to stretch minimal dollars to keep him and his siblings from losing the ranch, and keeping his brothers out of trouble, which had been an almost fulltime job in itself back when they'd been teens. The luxury surrounding him was as foreign to him as ordering a cappuccino-half-latte-soy instead of coffee.

He was not easily impressed...but damn. There was no way around it. He was totally knocked out by his cabin, his electric loaner car, the castle, and hell, the entire resort so far. In his wildest fantasies, he hadn't been expecting something like this.

He smiled. He loved that his three siblings had pulled together to pay for his vacation. For the next ten days, he had no responsibilities except to himself, and that felt a little surreal...kind of like this place. It'd been so long he since he'd relaxed and played, he hoped he remembered how.

After he unpacked, he took a long walk on the beach to stretch his legs. Hours on a horse were no problem, but he wasn't used to being cramped up in a tiny airplane row for most of a day.

When he'd begun to pack for the trip, he'd realized his supply of nice shorts and shirts had been, well, non-existent. That had been solved quickly when he'd taken a giddy Lauren to the Diamond Lakes Mall and turned her loose. Now, as he dragged his feet through the wet sand at the ocean's edge, he sported a crisp pair of khaki shorts and a new polo. He'd drawn the line, however, at her suggestion of tank tops and flip-flops. By the sparkle in her eyes, he'd been pretty sure—not positive, but pretty sure— she'd been kidding.

He said a quick prayer that they didn't burn down the house while he was gone.

The walk, a shower, and a quick nap took up most of his early evening. At eight-thirty when he awoke, he remembered the check-in clerk handing him a piece of paper about a beach party tonight. He found the informational flyer on the kitchen bar. He had plenty of time to get there. While he wasn't much of a partier, heading down to an evening party on the beach sure beat sitting alone in his cabin.

Fifteen minutes later, he bounded down his steps and stopped alongside the Model-T electric cart the resort had provided. He'd noted the bar's location today on his drive down to his cabin, and he debated walking there. It had to be less than a mile. But it was a warm night with measurable humidity so he opted to drive. No reason to get clean only to get sweaty again when he didn't have to.

The music was loud and reverberating off the water as he drove up to the welcome party. At least a hundred guests mingled in the outdoor bar, spilling onto the beach. A silvery, full moon and galaxy of stars glistened on ocean waves that continued their assault on the sand.

And women. Maybe it'd just been too long since

he'd been on a date, but everywhere he looked there was a beautiful woman.

Then one woman in particular sent his heart into overdrive. Seated at a table across the open-air room, she was in profile, but he remembered her from the Memphis airport and from check-in earlier. How could he miss her thick blonde hair spilling over her shoulders and down her back in waves? And her legs. Good lord. They went on for miles.

He made his way across the room, digging through his mental archives for a killer opening line. It'd been too long, and his mind was a blank slate. As he neared, he could see the smile twitching on her lips. Then he noticed she was stabilizing her cell-phone on the table and had it directed toward a male dancer dressed in a black Speedo and a Hawaiian shirt that had been left open, exposing a couple of gold chains around his neck.

He bent to speak directly into her ear. "He just doesn't look like your style."

She jerked back, pummeling his nose with the back of her head. "Oh! Ouch," she said, rubbing her head. An attractive pink tinge colored her cheeks. "I hope I didn't break your nose."

Worst opening line ever. Maybe his siblings were right. He did need to get out more.

He rubbed this throbbing nose. "Not broken. Or at least, I don't think so."

She frowned. "Um. Maybe you shouldn't be sneaking up on women you don't know."

"We can fix that." He held out his hand. "Brock Wade."

When she took his hand, he realized how soft her fingers were, unlike his, which were callused and rough from the ranch work. He might have held on a little too long after she straightened her fingers to finish the introductory handshake, but his flesh tingled from her touch, and he was reluctant to end the connection.

"Natalie Diamond." She smiled. "Are you sure I didn't break your nose?"

"I'm sure. I've had worse hits from my horse."

"So, you *are* a cowboy."

He dipped his head with a grin. Indicating the empty chair beside her, he asked, "May I?"

She shoved the chair out with her foot. "Please do."

Sitting, he said, "Got your eye on Mr. Speedo, do you?"

Her laugh hit him right in his gut with a solid punch. "He's one of those things you can tell your friends about, but without pictures, nobody is going to believe you."

"Get some good shots?"

She set her phone on the table, opened the camera app, and then scrolled through her quick snaps. She'd caught him in glorious color.

"I need a copy of those for my sister," he said. "She needs to see what kind of place she's sent me to."

Natalie snorted. "Forced vacation?"

37

"Sort of. Early Christmas present from my brothers and sister. You been here before?"

She shook her head. "Nope. Christmas present from my parents."

"Seems we have a lot in common."

She arched an eyebrow. "Families forcing us to take vacations for our own good?"

"Exactly," he said, more than pleased they were on the same wavelength. "Your glass is empty." He gestured toward her ice cubes in an otherwise empty glass on the table. "What are you drinking?"

"Maker's Mark on the rocks."

He hiked an eyebrow, intrigued now. He was a bourbon drinker, and it was rare that he had a woman to drink it with. Granted, he hadn't been dating much lately, but when he did, his dates always ordered beer or wine. He usually settled for a beer or wine to accommodate his date, but tonight?

"I believe I'll join you. Another?"

"Please."

He waved a harried cocktail waitress over and placed their orders. However, given the crowd, he ordered a double Marker's Mark for each of them with a side order of ice. He asked for their drinks to be served neat. No worrying about ice melting and diluting their excellent bourbon. That would allow them to drink at their leisure.

While they waited for their drinks, they discussed hometowns—Memphis, Tennessee for her and Diamond Lakes, Texas for him. Since he'd been to Memphis a time or two, they compared favorite restaurants, told some stories of famous person sightings there, and debated if the next earthquake would wipe out the Mississippi riverfront.

The waitress sat a bourbon in front of each of them, along with a second glass with only ice. Brock lifted his glass toward Natalie. She picked hers up, and they tapped drinks and resumed their earthquake discussion. As they drained the last drams of bourbon from this round, one of Brock's favorite Garth Brooks songs started. It was slow and perfect for a first dance with a fascinating woman.

"Dance?" He held out his hand. His question was met with a broad smile as she slipped her hand into his. The tingle he'd experienced before started again, an electric ripple that initiated at their joined hands and rolled up his arm before moving through his entire body.

They walked from under the bar's tiki-thatched roof and onto the sand. She kicked off her sandals, leaving them off to the side. He followed her lead, leaving his shoes beside hers. He slipped his arms around her waist while she looped hers around his neck. Holding her snugly against him, he began to move her to the slow tempo of "If Tomorrow Never Comes."

He drew in a deep breath, taking in the aroma of vanilla and oranges from the strands of her hair that'd landed under his nose. At six-foot-three, Brock almost always had to assume an uncomfortable bend to accommodate the height of his female dance partners. But not so with Natalie. Her head rested comfortably on his shoulder, and, for that, his back thanked his lucky stars.

When she hummed quietly along with the tune, he pulled her tighter against him, insanely pleased that she knew the song, which was totally ridiculous on his part. Still, he tightened his hold, pressing her full breasts against his chest. His heart galloped a little faster, and it wasn't because of the song's tempo. How crazy was it that here he was, thousands of miles from home, and the one woman who tripped his trigger lived only a little over nine hours from him?

She had to know he was attracted. Hell, the evidence was cradled between them. Even as the thought occurred, he felt his cock growing harder, but she didn't pull away. Instead, she moved in, letting him know she knew.

Slipping his leg between hers, he moved her slowly around the sandy dance area. Sadly, he knew the song well enough to recognize the final musical notes.

The next song had an upbeat tempo that didn't require holding on to Natalie and, damn, he hated the feeling of separation as he pulled his arms away. She seemingly felt the same as her limbs untwined slowly from him. As they moved apart, she gave him a smile that sent all his blood rushing from his head to below his waist. Then she laughed and whirled around, shaking her luscious booty to the beat of the music.

Brock laughed and danced, two actions that'd been sorely lacking in his life for years. But this woman made him feel like he was eighteen again, with his whole life ahead of him, instead of a thirty-two-year-old man with all his family obligations.

The next couple of songs were fast, but as soon as the slow tempo of "Let's Make Love" started, they moved together as though drawn by magnets. As they wrapped arms around each other, he danced her off into an area with less lighting. Her head rested on his shoulder, her breaths puffing soft caresses of air on his neck. He wanted to kiss her. Hell, needed to kiss her, but he wasn't sure how she would react.

Nonetheless, as they reached a shadowed spot, he lifted her chin with his fingers until their gazes met. Her breath caught as she looked into his eyes. He leaned forward and gave her a soft kiss. When she didn't pull away, he went back for a second, and then a third taste of her mouth. As their lips met for the third time, she moved closer, and her mouth opened slightly. Brock took advantage to sweep his tongue through the opening and into the heat of her mouth.

They shared breaths as the kiss got deeper and wetter, until he finally pulled away and rested his forehead on hers.

"Damn, woman." His heart kicked like a mule against his chest. "Your mouth is like a drug. I can't get enough."

He wrapped his hand around the back of her neck, threaded his fingers into her satiny hair, and sealed his lips to hers again. At the same time, he walked her backwards, deeper into the dark niche he'd found for them.

~

Natalie's legs quaked with nervous sexual attraction, so weak, she feared they wouldn't hold her upright. Brock Wade's kisses were like sin and heaven rolled into one. His tongue slipped into her mouth to stroke and taste everywhere. Their tongues twisted together, their individual tastes mingling until Natalie wasn't sure where she stopped and Brock started.

She let him back her into a dark corner, fully aware of what she was doing. Fun Natalie was in control now, completely shutting down any possible protests from Accountant Natalie. The area between her thighs grew hot and swollen with unresolved arousal. A whirl of heavy-duty lust spun in her gut, and she pressed her achy sex against his hard cock.

Finally, sanity forced its way to her brain's forefront. What was she doing? She barely knew this guy, and yet her body burned with need for him. She hadn't had sex since her divorce two years ago. She wanted sex. She missed it. Craved it. Wasn't that what she'd promised herself? A wild and crazy time?

But she didn't know this guy.

Her body didn't seem to mind that fact, but still...

She lost her train of thought as he ran the tip of his tongue around the rim of her ear, and then down the large tendon in her neck. He worked his way back up with kisses and nibbles. Chills marched down her spine, as fire leapt from nerve ending to nerve ending.

Grabbing his ass with both hands, she pulled his hardness against her. His butt was tight and firm, and, heavens, she wanted to touch the flesh there.

His hand slid up her ribs until it brushed the underside of her breast. She moaned low in her throat and fought the urge to shift until his palm covered her breast completely.

From somewhere deep inside, she found the resolve to stop this. She was minutes from screwing him right here on the beach within feet of other people.

She moved her hands to his waist and pushed him a couple of steps back until they were no longer touching.

"I'm sorry," he said with a strained voice. "I totally lost my mind."

She smiled and realized their breaths were coming in heavy pants. "Yeah. I know what you mean." Taking another step backwards, she said, "It's late. I was up early this morning, and I think my brain is a little fried."

He nodded. "Me, too. Can I walk you to your car?"

"I'd like that."

They found their shoes and walked to the small sandy parking area.

"This is me," Natalie said, stopping alongside her miniature Corvette.

Brock chuckled. "Cute." Hiking his thumb toward a black Model-T, he said, "I'm the black truck."

Natalie gave a little laugh. "I do love these cars. What a clever way to get around the resort."

"I agree."

They stood facing each other for a minute, both waiting for a signal from the other. Finally, Natalie said, "It's late. I'd better go."

Her heart sank in disappointment. She didn't really want to go, even though her rational mind knew it was the right thing to do. She wanted him to ask her to stay a little longer or maybe dip his head down and give her another of those kisses that made her toes curl.

"Okay. Thanks for the dance." Brock took a tiny step toward his car.

"My pleasure." She slid onto the seat of her electric car.

"Natalie." His deep voice rattled in his chest and sent an arrow of lust into her gut.

She looked up at him.

"Will you have dinner with me tomorrow night?"

The butterflies in her gut took flight as her mouth turned up into a grin. "I'd love to."

His face lit up with a smile. "Great. Here? Seven?"

She nodded. That sounded safe. A public place, just in case he was a serial killer or something. If she'd learned nothing else from her past two years of singlehood, she knew it was smart to meet strange men in public places.

He leaned in and kissed her. "I'll see you tomorrow then."

Natalie backed out of her space and headed for her cabin. In the rearview mirror, she watched Brock climb into his electric truck and pull in behind her. He followed her until she pulled over to the side.

"Are you following me?" she asked with a grin.

"I'm not, but where are you going? What cabin are you in?"

"Twenty-three. Where are you?"

"Twenty-one. Seems we're neighbors."

"Race you home," she said, and slammed her pedal to the floor. The Corvette leapt forward and charged down the lane. Behind her, she could hear Brock's laughter.

Five

Brock rolled over in bed, his internal alarm going off at its usual four a.m. The darkness outside filled the slit in the drapes. He shut his eyes, but they popped back open. Years of habit were impossible to break overnight. He swung his legs over the side of the bed and looked at the clock. Caribbean time was an hour later, so it was actually five instead of four. He threw on a pair of jogging shorts, a T-shirt, and his running shoes and headed for the road. At home, most of his exercise came from the daily ranch grind, and he missed the simple joy of running.

The crunch of shoes in the sand of the unpaved road broke the quiet of the morning. A smile crept onto his lips as Natalie Diamond jogged up.

"You're up early," he said.

"I could say the same about you." She continued to jog in place as she spoke.

"Just starting or finishing?"

She laughed. "At this hour, starting. Want to

come?"

"Sure. How far are you going?" he asked, as they began a slow jog up the road.

"I usually do about five miles. I haven't clocked anything here so I guess I'll go up to the castle and back, which should be at least three miles. You?"

"Don't get to run much anymore. Too much to do around the ranch. By the time I'm done for the day, I'm done, if you know what I mean."

She nodded. "Yeah, I know what you mean. I sit all day so if I didn't run or do something, my ass would be as wide as the Grand Canyon."

He dropped back to study her backside. "Looks good, in my opinion."

Laughing, she turned and ran backwards a couple of steps. "Stop that, and get back up here." She turned back around, and he was at her side within a couple of strides.

They ran up to the castle, and then past it, onto a road that led down the other side of the resort. The cabins here appeared larger, with more ornate external features.

"I think we've jogged into the rich neighborhood," Natalie whispered, echoing his own thoughts.

"My thoughts exactly." He pointed past one of the cabanas. "That one has a boat. Do you think it comes with the place or what?"

"No clue but, wow! What a boat." She looked over at him. "Are you a boating kind of guy?"

He smiled. "Fishing mostly. Used to ski, but those days are long past. You?"

"Love it. I adore the rock and sway of a boat. I went on a cruise a few years ago. I was afraid I would get sick, but nope. I was in heaven the entire time." She looked at him. "You ever been on a cruise? The food is incredible."

He shook his head. "Nope. I'm embarrassed to say this is the first vacation I've been on in quite a while. Ready to turn around?"

"Sure."

They started back toward the main resort.

"Got breakfast plans?" he asked.

Her lips arched up into a smile that he knew he'd never get tired of seeing. "I don't know. Do I?"

"You do. Breakfast with me at Surfside. Race you."

"You're on," she said and kicked in her boosters, leaving him behind.

He caught up with her as she jogged in place next to the moat bridge.

"This was loser buys, right?" she asked with a laugh. Being as this was an all-inclusive resort, the cost of meals was included in the daily rate.

"I think I can afford that."

They found a table on the stone terrace. The umbrella had been extended, which kept the glare from the rising sun off their faces. They weren't alone, as there were two other tables occupied at the moment. But the expansive area spread the diners apart, giving each table plenty of privacy.

The breakfast buffet stretched along one wall and, from what Brock could see, included every breakfast item a guest could want. A chef at the end would prepare a fresh omelet or waffles upon request. Otherwise, eggs, biscuits, bacon, sausage, ham, muffins, English muffins, bagels, breakfast potatoes, and a variety of fruit and yogurt filled the span.

He loaded his plate with an everything-but-the-kitchen-sink omelet, bacon, sausage, biscuits, and potatoes. If he ate all this, he'd be jogging twice a day. As he rejoined Natalie, he noted her simple meal of yogurt and fresh fruit.

"Is that all you're eating?" He waved a waiter over to request coffee.

She flipped her coffee cup over as a signal to the waiter. "This is my usual when I'm home," she said. "Most mornings, I'm in a rush after my run to get dressed and to work." Glancing back to the buffet, she added, "But now that I think about it, I'm heading back for the Belgian waffle calling my name."

Over breakfast, she asked about his family and ranch. They talked about the changing cattle industry—of which she knew very little—and ideas he had about increasing production. She was sympathetic to his financial woes and emotionally touched by his parents' unexpected deaths and his raising of his siblings.

He was surprised to discover that she'd had riding lessons as a teen.

"I loved the riding," she explained, "but we lived in the city. Stabling a horse in our backyard might have upset the neighbors."

He laughed. "But think of all the fertilizer you

could've offered them."

"Yeah, well, I don't think old lady Painter would've enjoyed having a horse eating her prize roses."

"Couldn't you have stabled a horse close by?"

"Sure, but you know how teen girls are. We're on to the next thing on a whim."

Brock thought about Lauren and nodded. He'd been through lots of "but Brock, everybody else is doing it," phases with her.

"So how long did you ride?"

"I took lessons and rode for about four years. Then I made cheerleader, and all my focus went there."

"I bet you looked great in that short cheerleading skirt."

Natalie laughed. "Those were short, that's for sure."

"Can you still do a cartwheel?"

"You betcha, and the splits, too."

He grinned at the mental picture forming in his head. "I think I'd like to see that."

"Not enough bourbon on the island," she replied with a chuckle.

"So, what are your plans for today?"

"Hmm. Well, I have a hot date tonight, but that's about it."

"A hot date? That sounds promising."

She hiked an eyebrow. "Could be."

"How would you like to do something crazy today?"

CYNTHIA D'ALBA

"Crazy like what?" She lifted her coffee mug to her mouth. Just watching her lips wrap around the cup's rim made him lose his train of thought. "Brock? Crazy, like how?" she repeated.

He cleared his throat. "Parasailing."

Her eyes opened wide. "Like up in the air?"

"Yeah. I've always wanted to, and I noticed that it's available here. But I'd love some company."

He could almost see the cogs and gears of her brain grinding, churning through the pros and cons. Truth be told, he'd dragged up the idea just because he wasn't ready to leave her side yet. She was funny and sexy, and he was having a hell-of-a-good time talking to her.

She nodded. "I'm scared to death, but let's do it."

Two hours later, they climbed into a speedboat along with another couple. The driver took them away from land and obstacles before slowing the boat.

With assistance, Natalie climbed into the leg openings of the harness. The guy helping her pulled them up her legs to her hips, and then secured the waist strap. A flare of something—jealousy maybe— stabbed Brock. He didn't want another guy's hands on Natalie.

But then the same resort employee helped him. When he noticed the routine for him was identical to the actions taken with Natalie, he had to laugh a little at himself.

"Okay," the boat assistant said. "Up here." He indicated a large platform at the rear of the boat. "You don't have to do anything. Just sit back, and you'll be lifted off."

Brock would never admit to anyone that his legs were a little shaky climbing onto the deck. He'd been the one to suggest this. He put on his I'm-not-scared face and stepped up.

Natalie took his extended hand and stood beside him. She looked at him, licked her lips, and said, "Here goes nothing."

The boat's speed accelerated, and they gently lifted. Brock had expected a jerk or pulling sensation, but it was more akin to floating upward. As the boat sped up, the assistant let out more of the line tethering them. The boat looked smaller and smaller as they climbed higher and higher.

Natalie let out a loud laugh. "I love it. Oh my God! It's like flying without a plane."

He smiled at her. "Not what I expected at all. You?"

"Nope. Better. Much better. Better than sex."

Brock arched his eyebrows. "Nothing's better than sex. I'd say you haven't had the right partner...yet."

She giggled and looked away, a blush tinting her cheeks. "Maybe."

Her reply was soft, but it was so quiet up in the air, he could hear everything. He reached over, took her hand, and squeezed.

"Look." He pointed to his left. A pod of dolphins swam below them, rising and dipping in the ocean's swells.

"How high are we?" Natalie asked.

"I read we'd go to about five hundred feet. I'm thinking we're probably at the end of our rope."

"Feels like we are a mile in the air. Look. You can see the Sand Castle from here."

For the next twenty minutes, they held hands, floated in the air, and pointed out fish and islands to each other. There were other boats in the area but none close to where their boat was cutting through the water. Brock decided this must be what heaven was like...holding hands with a beautiful woman high above all the world's chaos, without a care. Quiet and calm. So different from his real life where everyone, and everything, needed him, and it seemed like all at the same time.

The flying time was over too quickly. As the crew reeled them back into the boat, the ocean rose quickly to meet them. Natalie had asked the boat captain to skim them along the water as they came in for the landing. He did just that, lowering them to right above the waves, close enough they could dip their feet in. Natalie screamed with laughter as Brock caught a swell just right and was able to splash her.

But, too quickly they were lifted off the water and reeled back to the platform on the boat. Natalie's smile was so wide and so happy that Brock had to laugh.

"Have fun?"

The boat crew unharnessed them, and Natalie threw her arms around Brock's neck.

"Ohmygod, Brock. That was so awesome. I feel like I'm high."

He caught her around her waist and hugged her. "Good. I don't know if I enjoyed the flying or holding your hand more."

She rolled her eyes at his comment, but then winked at him.

He helped her off the deck so the next couple could take their turn. He dropped onto one of the cushions and pulled Natalie next to him. As the next couple prepared to take flight, Natalie unfastened her life jacket, wrapped her arms around his waist, and snuggled in.

"I'm not sure how I'll be able to top today," she said into his ear.

Her southern drawl and warm breath hit the tingle button on his nerves. She was the sexiest woman he'd met in ages. If only the real world wouldn't come crashing back in nine short days.

"Oh, I can think of a few ways to top today's high," he said.

She giggled and kissed him. Her lips were soft and warm, and his cock responded immediately. He shifted a little to give more room to the crotch of his shorts.

The water the boat was cutting through was fairly calm, but occasionally they would hit a wave. When that happened, Natalie's full breasts, covered in a rocking orange bikini bra, would slide up and down his arm and chest. It was the most delicious torture he'd felt in ages.

Six

꩜

Natalie watched the other couple high in the air and finally understood the old saying "high as a kite." She might have been out of the air and in the boat for ten minutes or so, but the adrenaline rush from soaring so high in the air still crashed through her veins. Her heart continued to race. Her breaths came in shallow pants. The ocean air smelled sweeter; the sun brighter. Her muscles jumped with excess energy. She felt strong and invincible, as though she was completely in charge.

She chuckled to herself with comprehension. This feeling, this mind-blowing high was why daredevils did crazy stunts. This feeling was why professional athletics drove themselves to do grueling workouts to remain physically fit and ready for a game. Even though she realized parasailing wasn't really that dangerous, she now craved that insane blast of energy again. And she had an idea who could do that for her.

Out of the corner of her eye, she studied the man she was holding on to. The muscles in his arms were like stone, and when he moved, his forearms became chiseled slabs of hard granite. His shoulders left her breathless! Broad and toned and—she mentally grinned—in need of some serious tanning. Brock had the infamous "farmer's tan" she'd always heard about. Tanned from mid-biceps down. She actually found it cute. Plus, she was glad he hadn't run to a tanning salon to even out his coloring like some men might have done. She loved that he was comfortable in his own skin, even if his legs hadn't seen any sunlight in at least four months.

The driver cut the boat into a turn, and they bounced over the wake left by another boat in the area. She bounced on the seat cushion, and her bikini-covered boobs wrapped themselves around Brock's arm. Gad. She'd have been embarrassed if he hadn't grinned like the devil when he felt them.

"Please refasten your life jackets," the boat captain instructed.

As she did, Brock leaned over and said into her ear, "Damn it. I was kind of enjoying that."

They arrived back at the Sand Castle Resort in the middle of the afternoon. The adrenaline rush had worn off. That combined with the energy-sapping hot sun had left her depleted. She needed a shower and a nap, in that order.

Brock jumped from the boat onto the pier, and then helped her make that transition. Once on the pier, he kept hold of her hand, and she really liked how that felt. His hands were large and warm and a little rough from work. She didn't mind the roughness and in fact, found it kind of sexy. Her ex-husband had gotten manicures and had always made sure his hands were soft and smooth. Sometimes, his hands had been more groomed than her own, and that had done awful things to her ego. But then, the entire marriage had been a total slap to any self-confidence she might have had about her appearance.

They climbed into Brock's mini-truck and started across the island to their cabins.

"I'm bushed," Natalie admitted. "I'm crashing from my high."

"Ditto." He glanced over at her and then back to the road. "But we're still on for dinner, right?"

"Oh yeah. Seven, right?"

"How about I pick you up?"

Natalie checked the time on her phone. It was only two, so that gave her plenty of time to rest up for tonight. "That works. Want me to just walk over to your place?"

He looked aghast. "Absolutely not. This is a date. I'm picking you up."

She chuckled. "Works for me."

At seven, Brock knocked on Natalie's door. When she opened it, her heart did a little stutter and she almost fell over in lust. Brock's hair was still a little damp from his shower. He wore a pair of crisp khaki shorts that Natalie suspected were new. A lemon-yellow, short-sleeve Henley stretched across his broad chest and shoulders. The shirt did wonderful things to highlight the developed muscles of his chest and arms. It was all she could do to not lick her lips in appreciation.

"Hi," he said, leaning a forearm on the door jamb. "Ready?"

"I am."

They got into his truck and drove about two hundred feet, where he pulled into the parking spot for cabin twenty-one.

"We're here," he said with a smile.

"Long drive," she joked. "I'm exhausted."

"I hope you don't mind, but I had dinner brought in. Breakfast at the restaurant was great, but I wanted to spend a little quiet time with you. That okay?"

Okay? Hell, it was fabulous.

"Sounds like a great plan."

His terrace was similar to hers in that it wrapped around one side of the cabana and then across the back. His view of the ocean was much the same. However, his terrace sported a cushioned two-person recliner, something hers didn't. A gentle glow from burning candles flickered in the salty breeze coming in off the ocean. The sun had long since set, replaced by a full moon and a full galaxy of stars. Palm fronds and tropical trees swayed in the breeze, making shadows dance on the terrace floor and walls.

"This is lovely, Brock," Natalie said.

"I didn't ask what you liked to eat. Sorry. I had to take a stab at it. Hope I got something you like."

She smiled. "I'll eat just about anything, except liver."

"Whew. Thank goodness. Liver was on my list, but I marked it off at the last minute."

She laughed.

"Would you like a drink? I have bourbon, but also wine if you'd prefer it."

"I'll stay with what I know."

"Bourbon, it is. I left it in the kitchen."

She followed him into his cabana and to his kitchen. Like her place, his was professionally decorated with comfortable, tropical-themed furniture. The kitchen was almost identical to hers with its apartment-sized appliances. A tantalizing aroma of spices and herbs filled the air.

"Smells wonderful."

He looked over his shoulder. "Dinner is in the oven on low. Ready to eat when we are. Are you hungry now?"

Maybe, but not for the food you're offering.

"I think a drink first might be nice, but I'll get it. Can I pour you one?"

"Sure. Thanks."

Natalie stepped up to the kitchen island and cracked the top on a new bottle of Maker's Mark. As she poured, a pair of warm, strong arms wrapped around her from behind. She leaned back against the rock-solid chest pressed up to her back. Brock kissed her neck. She rocked her head to the side to give him better access. His lips caressed the skin below her ear, and a shiver slithered down her spine. When he ran the tip of his tongue down the tendon in her neck and then nibbled his way back up to her chin, her toes curled. This man had a wicked mouth and knew what to do with it.

He put his hands on her waist and turned her until she was surrounded in his arms. Their gazes met and held. Natalie caught his face in the palms of her hands and pulled him down to her. His tongue eased between her lips and filled her mouth. His deep-chested groan ignited a volley of fireworks in her gut.

She slid the palms of her hands to his chest, enthralled by the twitches and jumps of his muscles when she flexed her fingers. Between the peaks and valleys of tendons and sinew, she felt not an ounce of excess flesh. She pushed her hands under the tail of his shirt and lifted.

"I want to see what I'm feeling." She blurted out the words without thinking, but there was no way to suck them back. Her heart gave a rapid and almost painful kick to her sternum. Why had she said that? Would he think she was nuts?

But the smile that slowly spread across his face had her heart jumping for all the right reasons. Brock lifted his arms above his head, and Natalie pushed the Henley up and off. Her knees almost gave out at the sight. Thick muscles bulged on his chest and biceps. His abdomen looked like a snow mogul course, and of course she skied her hands down it. Bump. Dip. Bump. Dip. Her head swam with lust.

"You should model," she said, continuing to run the palms of her hands over the male perfection in front of her.

He laughed. "Not hardly, but thank you."

"I'm serious, Brock. You are..." She couldn't finish her sentence. Instead, she leaned over and placed a kiss over his heart. Even as she did, her fingers played on the mogul course below.

"You're playing with fire," he warned in a gravelly voice.

"Maybe I'm a secret pyromaniac." She licked his nipple and watched it harden.

He groaned. "Worst kept secret ever."

If she licked his nipple again, he was going to throw her over his shoulder, caveman-style, and haul her straight to his bed. To heck with finesse. Lust roiled in his gut like a dragon waking up after being asleep for a couple hundred centuries. Once awake, it demanded to be fed.

"I'm feeling a little underdressed," he said, slipping his hands under her shirt. His fingers flexed against her warm, soft flesh. Her breathing quickened as he glided his hands up her ribcage until the backs of his fingers brushed the underside of her breasts.

He got a glimpse of her dilated eyes before she shut them and gave herself over to his ministrations. The corners of his lips twisted up as the dragon inside shot flames of desire through his veins. He pulled his hands back until he reached the shirt's hem and began lifting it over her head. He moved slowly, giving her time to protest or object. Instead, she mimicked him and raised her arms over her head to facilitate removal.

There was hardly any blood remaining in his brain for rational thought. It seemed that every drop had collected below his waist. His dick strained at his zipper as though demanding to be released.

Once her shirt was gone, he got his first glimpse of her peach-colored lace bra. His knees went a little unsteady at the vision of this beautiful blonde in front of him with her eyes closed, a Mona Lisa smile on her mouth, and her full, luscious breasts moving sensually up and down with each breath. That changed when he covered each breast with a hand. She drew in a deep breath and let it out in a long, stuttering sigh.

"You're so beautiful," he said, and lowered his mouth to one lace-covered nipple. He sucked her through the material while he plucked the other breast with his fingertips.

Her heart pounded against his lips. He had to taste her...now. He pushed the bra up, and her fleshy breasts fell into his hands. Caressing and squeezing them had the last ounce of blood in his body racing to his cock. His dick was hard enough to drive fence posts...into dry, Texas dirt.

He lowered his mouth to her flesh and sucked. She groaned and reached out to stroke him through his shorts. There was no way he was going to be able to move slowly, to take his time seducing her. He wanted to be inside her. Wanted to feel her velvet channel surrounding him.

Something vibrated against his groin and interrupted his thoughts.

Ignore it, his cock demanded.

But Natalie gently pushed him away. "I'm sorry. I need to answer that. My parents are on their first cruise, and they promised to call when they made port." She shrugged and gave him an apologetic look. "Sorry."

Brock stepped back. Natalie pulled her phone from her shorts and answered without taking her eyes off his chest.

"Hello?"

Her face solidified into irritation with a shade of anger. Her sexy, playful voice changed into a no-nonsense, stern inflection.

"Well, I'm sorry," she said, her back to him. As she spoke, she pulled her bra back into place. "I can't help it if Bambi found someone younger, richer, and better looking." She paced across the living room to stare out the windows overlooking the ocean. "Tiffany. Bambi. Whatever. Look, Tim, I'm sorry for you. Really, I am, but no. *No*. I'm not sending you any money so you can fly to Memphis." She laughed, but it wasn't one of amusement. "I don't care if she's jealous of me. I really don't give a flying fart what you or she thinks or wants."

Brock found his shirt and slipped it back over his head.

"No, I'm not coming to California either. We're

divorced. We've been divorced for two years." There was a pause in the conversation. "That's ridiculous. I'm not your lodestar. You need to find someone else to ground you instead of me. No. No. I mean it, Tim. Stop calling."

Her shoulders sagged, and she blew out a long sigh. "Yes, that's the way it has to be."

She clicked off her phone and shoved it back in her pocket.

"Nothing like a bucket of cold water to put out a fire," she said, still staring out the window. "Sorry to have ruined the evening." Finally, she turned to face him. "You don't have to see me home."

The sexual flush that'd colored her cheeks was gone. The Mona Lisa smile had been replaced with a sad, apologetic one.

His raging erection had sagged to half-mast as he realized this evening had just taken a different turn.

"I'm sorry, Brock. I shouldn't have answered the call."

He poured two fingers of bourbon and walked it over to her. "Of course, you had to answer it. Drink this, and then we'll have dinner."

Her brow furrowed. "You still want to have dinner?"

"Prime rib with all the fixings. And Key Lime Pie for dessert. Take it or leave it." He kissed her. "Stay. I'd like you to."

She downed the bourbon. "I'd like to stay. Thank you."

Seven
⟶⟵

Natalie lay in bed, not wanting to move. But after last night's dinner and pie, her ass would require an entire row of seats on the plane home if she didn't run. She looked at the clock. Five-forty-five.

Throwing her legs over the side of the bed, she sat up with a long sigh. Where were her mother's awesome thin genes? Unfortunately, Natalie had inherited her paternal grandmother's love of cooking and sweets, along with her propensity for fat storage in her butt and thighs.

Last night had been, well, incredible, up until Tim had called. She'd been prepared for questions, but Brock hadn't asked. They'd had dinner, talked about everything except for the elephant in the room, and she'd appreciated his lack of inquiry.

After slipping on a clean shirt, shorts, and jogging shoes, she headed out to face the slog around the resort. Her heart leapt, and she stopped short when she came across Brock sitting on her bottom step. Damn. How did that man look so delicious at this freaking early hour?

"What are you doing here?"

Brock stood, his pristine white T-shirt straightening and stretching over all those muscles she'd had the pleasure of touching last night. "Waiting for you." He gave a pointed look at his watch and then back to her. "Running a little late this morning, are we?"

She laughed. "*We* are not wanting to run at all this morning, late or not."

"Me neither, and that's why I'm here. I needed the foot in the ass to get going."

She jumped off the bottom step and deepened her voice. "Okay, buddy. Let's get a move on. Daylight's a-burning."

They started their run out on a slow jog. The sand and shell covering cracked and shifted with each step.

"I enjoyed dinner last night," Natalie said. "Thanks, again."

"Me, too. You interested in trying it again, only maybe this time without the phone?"

She lost a step then got back into rhythm. "Yeah, sorry about that."

"You ready to talk about it?"

Not ever, was what she wanted to say. Instead, she said, "It's hard to explain, but I'll try."

As they ran, she told him her life story. About meeting Tim Evers in high school, and how they'd been together every day until their divorce. Tim had been her first everything. She'd loved him, but he'd grown up in a family of boys with no maternal influence. He craved female attention. Loved to flirt. They'd broken up in college for a week, but he'd come back, begging her to marry him. She had, and for a while, everything had been cake and ice cream.

But then she'd discovered Tim had been having an affair with a woman from work. He'd sworn it'd never happen again, so Natalie had taken him back. Of course, a tiger can't change his stripes.

The next time Natalie found out about an affair she'd kicked him out. Tim had been remorseful, begging and, like a fool, she'd taken him back. It wasn't that Natalie was opposed to divorce as a concept, but she'd given the majority of her years to a relationship with Tim and she'd wanted the dream marriage.

They'd moved to Southern California to give the marriage a fresh start. Tim had found God and dragged her to one of the mega-churches week after week. For about eighteen months, things had seemed fine but...

She looked at Brock. "That old tiger-stripes issue. But this time, Tim was having an affair with the preacher's daughter."

"And this would be Bambi?"

Natalie actually laughed and it felt good. "No, it was Honey. The girl's actual name is Bertilia Imelda Godbehere."

"You're kidding, right?"

"Nope. Named after saints. Anyway, she was so sweet that everyone called her Honey."

Brock made a gagging sound, which caused Natalie to snort when she laughed.

"Yeah. Me, too. Anyway, Honey has gotten used to having money and spending it like she printed it herself. Tim has pretty much gone through every penny he has, and Honey is getting the roving eye, which is, of course, sauce for the gander. He wanted to come to Memphis or me to come to Southern California to make Honey jealous, so she'd take him back. Yeah, that's not gonna happen."

"When did you move to Memphis?"

"After the divorce. Moved into the family home, and my parents headed south for a beachfront condo and the good life."

"Can I say that your ex-husband is not only an ass, but a fool?"

"Sure. I say it all the time."

"And so, the ex is in the past?"

"Oh God, yes. We're done. He knows that, but he was pretty drunk and desperate last night."

Brock didn't say anything, which made Natalie nervous. She knew some guys steered away from divorced women. But she'd done nothing to cause her marriage to fail. If anything, she'd forgiven him too many times and had stayed way past the marriage's expiration date.

Gathering her courage to take his rejection like an adult, Natalie asked, "Does it bother you that I'm divorced?"

He shook his head. "Nope. Just thinking about how very stupid your ex must be to have left you for another woman."

Relief at his response flooded her heart. "Thank you."

By now they'd passed the castle and into an area they'd learned was a small community of exclusive private homes.

"When I was booking the parasailing yesterday," Brock said, "the gal at the reservation deck told me about a path that almost nobody knows about. It's open to the public, but it's so close to the private area that it's pretty much overlooked. She said to look for a blue rock on the right just past the house with the red tile roof."

Natalie giggled. "Have you looked at these houses? They all have red tile roofs."

And they did. Nonetheless, Natalie spotted the rock, and they turned right. The path led out to a shaded lane that ran along the beach. Fresh sea air rolled in with the waves crashing on shore. Birds flew above the azure water, diving periodically for a fish meal.

"This is beautiful."

Brock grunted. "Yeah, but this loose sand is hell to run in. Let's back off the pace a little and enjoy the view."

Natalie immediately dropped to a walk. Propping her hands on her waist, she sucked in air. "I thought you'd never ask."

After a couple of minutes of silent walking,

Natalie asked, "What's on your agenda for today?" She pulled her T-shirt up and wiped her sweaty face.

He mimicked her action. "Whatever you're doing, if that's okay with you...?"

"Well..." She wrinkled her nose. "I was going to go to the beach for some sun, and while you're welcome to join me..." She took a pointed look at his white legs. "I am a little worried you'll fry like a chicken leg in grease."

She quit worrying that she'd offended him when he burst out laughing.

"What? Pasty white legs ain't your thang?"

She laughed.

"It's winter, babe. Jeans and boots all the time at home. But I'll be fine. My sister packed a bottle of SPF-50 in my suitcase...or maybe it's SPF-100. Not sure"

"Lauren, right?"

He nodded. "Right. She's been a ranch gal all her life. She knows what happens to the summer tans come winter."

"Race you back?" She started to jog in place.

They took off at a run back toward their cabins, but stopped for breakfast as they passed the castle. It was almost ten when Natalie walked over to Brock's cabin and knocked.

"Come in," he yelled.

She opened the door. "I'm headed down."

Brock came out wearing a pair of board shorts and a muscle shirt.

"Where's your SPF-50? We aren't leaving without it."

His cheeks tinged pink when he held up a bottle with the picture of a baby on it. "I'm going to kill my sister."

Natalie grinned. "Sounds like she was worried about your baby-smooth, delicate skin."

Brock laughed. "I don't want to talk about it. C'mon." He threw an arm around her shoulders. "And I rented us a tent cabana in case we start getting too much sun."

She snaked an arm around his waist. "What a great idea. Thanks."

The scent of soap and clean man swirled around her and made her squeeze in a little tighter.

When they got to the beach, there were a number of brightly striped canvas cabanas erected with sides that would raise or lower by a pulley. Each one had a sign attached. It didn't take long to find the one labeled Wade and Diamond. Conveniently, it was set up right behind Natalie's cabin.

Inside the cabana, the sand had been covered with an outdoor rug. Sitting on the rug were two beach recliners with cushions and two towels. Each chair had its own table. On one of the tables was a portable radio.

"Okay." Natalie looked around. "Now, I'm impressed."

Brock nodded. "They do it right here."

"What's the radio for?" Natalie pointed to the electronic device.

"Beachside service. If we need drinks or food or towels, we can call in, and someone will bring it down to us."

"Totally ridiculous. I love it."

"Want me to move your chair out into the sun?"

"Please. I'm not going to be out long. Want to come, or are you going to be smart and stay in the shade?"

"After you made fun of my legs? Ha," Brock said with a mock scowl. "I'm doing neither. I'm headed out to the ocean. You want to get wet?"

Natalie choked as her mind went to a totally inappropriate response. She swallowed hard. "I think I'll work on my tan."

He got her set up on the beach with her chair, towel, and the radio. When he stripped off his shirt to head to the water, she licked her lips. *Man-oh-man.* She had to figure out a way to see the rest of him.

Damn Tim. She might have had her chance last night if he hadn't called.

As Brock made his way to the water's edge, she noticed a number of other women in the area giving him decidedly lusty looks. The man could have any of those women with a flex of his finger...or his biceps. Why was he with her? There were better looking women here and many with much better figures than hers.

She watched him swim into the waves, his strong back muscles popping and bulging with each stroke. Damn, she was drawn to him. She had to stop staring at him before he caught her. She forced herself to lie back on the recliner and soak up some rays. Meanwhile, she let a little erotic fantasy run in her brain like a movie.

Cold water dripped on her chest. She screamed and sat up. Brock grinned at her. Around her, the wind had picked up considerably since they'd arrived on the beach.

"Storm's coming," Brock said.

Natalie rolled to her side and looked up into dark clouds. She frowned. "When did those roll in?"

"Just now. You were asleep. Thought we'd better—"

The skies took that moment to open the floodgate. Buckets of water poured over her head and body. Natalie jumped from her chair, laughing. A bolt of lightning hit the water, followed closely by a deafening roar of thunder. The wind howled around them, then whipped up sand, stinging her legs.

"We need to get inside and out of this," Brock shouted. He grabbed her hand. "Come on."

Around them, other guests were racing off the beach to shelter. Resort employees were scurrying to store chairs, umbrellas, and cabanas before they could be lifted into the ocean.

"Where's our cabana?" she asked as they jogged past the site where it had been earlier.

"Helped one of the guys take it down. I've been watching this storm coming on for a while. I wanted to let you get as much tanning as you could today since this storm will last the rest of the night."

"And you know this how?" she yelled over the wind.

"Years of watching storms. When you have cattle to take care of, you learn about things like that."

They hustled down the path toward Brock's cabin. By now, they were both drenched. There wasn't a square inch on Natalie that wasn't wet, and that pretty much entailed everywhere on her body. Brock's large hand wrapped around her fingers as he hurried toward his cabin. From her towed perspective, his tight ass looked downright fabulous. She jerked on his hand to get his attention.

"Slow down," she called. "We can't get any wetter."

He stopped and looked at her, and then smiled. "You're not like most women."

"How's that?"

"You're not freaking out that your hair's wet or that you've got mascara running down your face."

"I do?" She swiped at her cheeks, but her hand came back clean. Then she remembered she wore waterproof mascara.

He laughed and stepped up until her breasts were brushing his chest. Capturing her face between his hands, he attacked her mouth, licking and nibbling and sucking her tongue into his mouth. Her legs became so rubbery that it was a wonder she could stand.

She ran her hands up his chest, the feel of water sluicing down the firm muscles sending her mouth into a frenzy on his.

His hands slipped from her face and down her arms until he held her ass in the palms of his hands. He pulled her against the bulge in his board shorts. He didn't have to tug very hard. Natalie ground her aching groin against his hardness.

He leaned back until their gazes met. "I want you," he said. "I want you in my bed in every position we can think of. If you don't want that, speak now."

She pushed away, and disappointment flashed on his face. "Then why are we standing in this freaking rain?"

Eight

Natalie raced up the flagstone steps to the terrace with Brock close on her heels. He caught her as she reached the door and wrapped his arms around her, pressing his hard body to her back. He kissed the area below her ear, and she shivered.

"Cold?" he asked.

"No. Wait." She looked over her shoulder. "If I said yes, would I get a hot shower?"

A broad grin was his only reply. He opened the door, walked her through with him still plastered to her backside, then slammed the door behind them. He took her hand and led her through the cabin, through a bedroom larger and plusher than hers, into a bathroom that'd been conceived from her fantasies. The white marble tiled room was dominated by a glass-walled shower with multiple showerheads.

He swung her around until her back pressed against the marble counter then took her mouth in a crushing kiss of heat and tangled tongues. Walking his fingers up her back, he nimbly unhooked the bikini bra, releasing the tension around Natalie's chest. With his tongue dueling hers for control, he pushed the bra up, freeing her breasts into his work-roughened hands. Calloused fingers plucked her nipples, sending zinging electricity to her core. The harder he pinched and pulled, the more her sex throbbed. She swore she could feel it swelling in response to his nipple play.

He pulled away from the kiss long enough to strip her bra down her arms and turn on the shower. Water streamed from all the shower openings extending from the wall.

Now that the time was here, nervous uncertainty clawed at Natalie's confidence. What if Brock didn't like her body? Thought she was fat? It'd been over two years since she'd been with a man. What if she really sucked at this and that was why Tim had had affairs?

As though reading her mind, Brock trailed his fingers down her ribcage to her hips.

"You were made for this," he said, sliding his thumbs into the elastic of her bikini bottoms. "Your body is perfect." He took a nipple in his mouth and sucked. Natalie's head dropped back as a tingling wave of arousal formed an eddy in her gut.

He kissed the underside of her breast, running his tongue along the seam where her flesh met rib.

"God, you taste so good," he said in a gravelly tone.

Natalie pulled her head up and forward so she

could watch him working his mouth and tongue down her abdomen. When he got to her navel, he rimmed it with the tip of his tongue and then went to his knees as though worshiping a goddess.

The sight of this strong, virile man on his knees in front of her had her grabbing the counter's edge to remain upright.

His fingers dug into her hips as he took hold of the bikini's material. He pulled it slowly down her legs to the floor, then lifted one foot then the other to remove it. After tossing it over into the corner, he kissed her ankle. Then slowly, and with exquisite torture, he licked and kissed his way up her legs, alternately left, right, left, right. Each stroke of his tongue added to the intense swirling inside her gut.

By the time he reached the lips of her sex, she was quivering, wet, and desperate. Would he think her forward if she hopped on the counter and draped her legs around his neck?

It turned out that she didn't have to do anything.

"Spread your legs," he muttered, while tonguing the inside of her thigh.

Natalie spread her feet, but it wasn't enough to accommodate his broad shoulders.

"Wider," he said, then sucked the flesh at the junction of her hip and her thigh. He stopped sucking and looked up at her. "Wider, babe. Much wider. I want to see you while I enjoy the taste of you in my mouth."

Natalie could do the splits. That should be wide enough. She opened her legs. Brock's fingers made dents in the flesh of her hips as he held her and ran his tongue along the seam of her sex.

"Tastes so good." His tongue separated her folds, and he ran a long lick down one side and then the other. Using his thumbs, he pulled her vaginal lips apart, exposing her like she'd never been exposed before.

Tim hadn't liked oral sex, or at least giving it. However, he loved getting it.

But Brock? He seemed to be taking pleasure from giving her pleasure.

"Beautiful," he said. "Are you watching? Can you see my tongue as it fucks you like I'm going to do? Look to your right. Watch me tongue-fuck you." With that, he jabbed his tongue into her core, pulling it out and thrusting it in again and again.

Natalie turned her head and for the first time saw the full-length mirror. Saw herself standing spread-eagle. Saw a toned, muscular man on his knees at her feet. Watched as his tongue danced over her sex and in and out of her core.

Her knees grew weak. The eddy inside was spinning at hurricane force. The tension was so strong as to be almost painful. She sucked in her abdomen. Her pulse raced. Her breath came in pants and gasps. She moaned loudly.

"Damn, Brock. I'm going to come."

He stroked her with his tongue. "That's the idea, baby. Let it go. Let me watch you come apart."

Her thighs shook with muscular tension. She bent her knees as the internal pressure inside her climbed to a peak. Her entire body went taut, and then she was flying. Behind her closed eyes, bright white lights flashed and danced. Her abdominal muscles jumped and quaked. She screamed out his name.

When her orgasm had passed, she looked down into a very smug face.

"Liked that, did you?" Brock asked.

"Oh, it was all right." She could barely suppress the smile that tugged at the corners of her mouth.

He laughed, jerked off his shorts, and pulled her into the now steamy shower.

"Just all right? I guess I'll have to work harder next time."

Harder? Hell, that'd probably kill her!

For the first time, she got a look at his equipment, so to speak, and Lord have mercy. The moguls of his abdomen leveled out to a flat, tight stomach. A trail of dark hair led from his cute belly button (since when did she think belly buttons were cute?) down to a thatch of thick, dark hair. Arising from that nest of hair was a cock that made the only other one she'd ever seen look like a pencil. She licked her lips, then raised her head to look him in the eye.

"Damn, man. You are mighty fine," she gasped out.

He grinned and pulled her into a crushing hug. Warm water hit them from all angles. He took her mouth in a bruising kiss while slipping his hand between her legs. His fingers parted her folds and found the entry to her soul. He pushed in a thick finger and curved it to reach the most sensitive part.

She groaned her approval and pleasure at his touch.

A second finger joined the first, while he massaged her clitoris with his palm. She ground against his hand. Snaked a leg around his hip. Opened herself to him, physically and emotionally.

He pumped his fingers in and out of her, thrusting his tongue in and out of her mouth in the same pattern. She was overwhelmed with sensations. His thick fingers inside her, touching places that'd never been touched. His tongue filling her mouth, stroking everywhere inside. Hot water streaming down her back and between the crack of her ass. Her head swam as her brain was flooded with the erotic sensations Brock brought out of her.

An electrical storm lit up her insides and sent jolts of tingling charges through her veins. Powerful pressure built until she couldn't hold off any longer. Wave after delicious wave of ecstasy rippled through her body.

Brock backed her against a wall. "Hold on." He reached through the door and snagged a condom off the counter. Natalie's pulse jumped at the tear of the foil.

"Let me do it," she said.

"No way, babe. I'm almost at the edge right now."

She poked out her lower lip. "But I know how to do it with my mouth."

He hissed out a breath and rolled the condom down his rigid cock. "Don't tell me that. You're killing me."

"Not fair," she complained. "I didn't even get to touch you."

Cupping her ass in his hands, he lifted her feet off the shower floor. "You can next time. I may not let you out of my bed until we fly home."

"If that's a threat, you'll have to do better," she said and wrapped her legs around his hips. "Now, fuck me, cowboy." She couldn't believe those words came out of her mouth. Never had she been so crude, but if Brock's responding grin told her anything, it was that he loved it.

He poised the tip of his dick at her entrance and pushed in slowly. Her walls stretched to accommodate him. It felt wonderful, an itch that was finally getting scratched.

Pulling back, he thrust in again, going deeper. On the third thrust, he filled her completely. His balls spanked her ass with each pounding shove of his cock. The only sounds were wet flesh slapping against wet flesh and his grunts with each stroke. His fingers burrowed grooves into the globes of her bottom. Her back hit the glass wall and slid up with each commanding thrust of his rock-hard dick. She knew she wouldn't last long, and she didn't. Her orgasm hit her like a freight train. Hard and fast. She screamed.

Two hard thrusts later, Brock pushed in and held as his own climax hit. He filled her so completely that she could feel the pulse as he ejaculated.

Breathless, he dropped his head onto the wall next to her ear.

"Damn. Just..." He blew out a long breath. "Let me catch my breath."

She laughed and kissed him. "We're going to get pruney if we stay in here."

His chuckle was deep and vibrated her chest. "I'll soap you if you'll soap me."

"Deal."

As usual, Brock awoke early. Not as usual, there was an incredible woman in his bed. As Hank had said the morning Brock had received his early Christmas gift, Brock was more accustomed to bar hook-ups where he could leave as soon as the deed was done. That sounded so cold, now that he thought about it. But he'd always made sure the lady got what she needed too.

However, oral sex wasn't something he passed out like Valentine candy. With Natalie, he'd been almost frantic to taste her. She'd been like a drug. He wanted more. He craved more.

Beside him, a very naked Natalie Diamond lay curled on her side, her hand alongside her face. Her thick, blonde hair lay in waves and curls on the pillow. Her side dipped in at her waist then flared again at her hips.

He wanted to grab her, take her from behind, but

he'd had her three times more after they'd gone to bed, the last one being only a couple of hours ago.

This was crazy. She was making him crazy. Her laugh, her smile and, fuck, even wrapping one of the curls in her hair around his finger made his balls ache with need. His cock strained with a morning erection.

She drew in a deep breath and let it out. Her eyelids flickered open. She stared across the room for a moment then rolled to her back and looked up at him. A smile slowly stretched across her lips.

"Good morning," she said.

"Morning to you. Sleep good?"

She stretched her arms over her head, which pulled the sheet down, exposing her plump breasts. His cock, already stiff, grew painfully rigid at the sight.

"Hmm," she purred. "I feel wonderful."

He leaned over and caught her breast in his lips, sucking it hard and deep into his mouth, while rolling the nipple of her other breast between his fingers. He pulled her nipple, loving how it stretched and elongated at his touch.

Natalie threaded her fingers into his hair and pulled as she moaned and shifted her hips on the mattress. When she scratched her nails into his scalp, he sucked firmly on one nipple and pinched the other.

"God, that feels so good," she cried out. "Don't stop."

He didn't. Instead, he shoved the sheet down to

her knees, where he could catch it with his foot and jerk it off the bed. Then he slipped his free hand between her thighs and found her hot and wet and ready for him.

"Damn, woman," he growled. "You're so wet." He slid a finger up and down her cleft. "So fucking wet."

When he pushed three fingers inside, she arched up from the bed with a cry. She moved her hips back and forth as he slid in and out.

"That's right, Nat. Fuck my fingers. Come all over my hand."

She groaned and pumped herself on his fingers. A flush started on her chest and climbed up her neck to her cheeks. She was fucking beautiful as she strained to reach her climax. What someone like her was doing with a rough cowboy like him baffled him, but damned if he was going to ask any questions. Arousal fluid poured from her onto his hand, and he ached to suck her dry. When he pulled his hand from her, her head whipped up.

"What's wrong?"

The frantic look on her face made him laugh.

"Not a damn thing that my mouth on you won't fix."

He grabbed a pillow off the floor. "Lift your hips."

She did, and he crammed the pillow under them, raising her higher on the mattress. That put her at a perfect height for his mouth and his eyes.

He sucked her sex between his lips as he stabbed his tongue into her valley. Fluid gushed into his mouth as he drank from her. Shoving his hands under her ass, he slid his middle finger down her ass crack, and he wondered if she would stop him from fingering her there.

She didn't. Instead, she shifted slightly to give him better access to the opening.

He pressed his middle finger in up to his first knuckle. She gasped. She was tight, so tight he suspected anal play wasn't something she'd done often, if ever. He stopped everything and waited for a minute.

"You okay?"

"Yes," she grunted out as she pressed her ass down on his finger.

He pushed his finger in up to the middle knuckle. She hissed and then moaned.

He pulled his finger back and thrust it all the way in, roughly and firmly. She wiggled.

"Feel good?" he asked and ran his tongue around her clit.

"Can't. Speak," she gasped out.

He sucked her rigid nub into his mouth while he turned his finger in her ass. She bucked and cried out his name.

He pulled away from her long enough to slide on a condom, then drove his dick deep inside her. She was still coming. That realization punched him in the gut. She dug her heels into the bed and pushed as he pounded into her. Her second climax came quickly.

CYNTHIA D'ALBA

He lasted only one more stroke before he followed her over the edge.

As they lay with their limbs entwined, Brock's mind worked to understand the emotions flooding him. Emotions he hadn't expected and definitely emotions he hadn't felt for anyone other than family in a long, long time.

Nine

The days passed quickly. Too quickly. She only went back to her cabin for changes of clothes. She spent every night with Brock, in his bed, in his arms.

Today was December twenty-third, her last day with Brock. Natalie sighed and rolled onto her back. When she reached for him, the bed was empty, but that wasn't all that surprising. She'd discovered quite quickly that he rose with the chickens, as her grandmother used to say.

Pulling the covers up to her chin, she stared at the ceiling and thought about the past nine days. The entire vacation felt like the best erotic dream she had ever experienced.

Days had been ideal. Sunny. Mid-seventies. Light breezes.

The nights might have been fantasies, only she could have never dreamed these up. Her prior sexual experiences had consisted mostly of her giving Tim oral sex, him responding with a couple of minutes of foreplay, and then sex in the missionary position. *Wham. Bam. Thank you, Ma'am.*

Sex with Brock had opened her eyes to a whole new world. A world where she wasn't responsible for her own pleasure. A world where nothing was taboo. Her approach to life and love would never be the same. She was reborn and starting all over with love.

She pulled his pillow to her and wrapped her arms around it. How do you thank a man for opening you to new feelings? New realities?

And worse, how do you let go and forget a man like Brock Wade?

She had to. She knew that. This was a vacation fling. Pure and simple. Neither of them had asked the other for anything but a good time. He had delivered on that. She hoped he felt the same way.

In fact, she hoped he left with wonderful memories of their time together. While she could admit she wasn't ready for it to be over, that admission would only be to herself. Never to him. She didn't want to be the type of woman who clung like ivy to bricks to a guy just because they'd had sex.

"Morning, gorgeous."

If nothing else, Brock had been great for her self-esteem.

Her male fantasy stood in the doorway, a cup of coffee in each hand. She scooted up in bed.

"Coffee in bed. I could get used to this." Even as the words left her mouth, she wanted to suck them back. This was a vacation fling. They'd agreed to that.

That last thing she wanted was to imply that she'd changed the rules and now wanted something long-term. Luckily, Brock didn't seem to notice her poor choice of words.

"You know, this coffee could come with strings attached," he said, walking over to the bed.

Natalie hiked an eyebrow. "Such as?"

"I don't know yet. Naked bowling, maybe."

She burst out laughing at the image that formed in her mind. "That might not be a pretty sight."

He grinned and handed her a cup. His face sobered. "Our last day."

Her pulse kicked up a notch at his words. He'd realized it, too.

"I know." She sipped the black gold from the cup and sighed. "They do have the best coffee here."

He hip-bumped her. "Scoot over."

When she did, he sat on the mattress, leaned against the headboard, and stretched out his legs.

"So, what's on the agenda today?" Natalie asked. "Parasailing again? Jet skis? Shopping? Yacht ride around the harbor?"

He laughed at the last one. "No yachts." His face got pensive. "A last ride around the resort, a nice dinner catered to the terrace, and you by my side. That's what I want for today."

She dropped her head onto his shoulder, still amazed at the powerful muscles there, and sighed. "Sounds lovely."

He wrapped his hand around the back of her head and pulled her over for a kiss.

"Breakfast on the beach?" he asked.

"Of course. Give me ten minutes." She slipped from the bed and raced to the bathroom.

When she joined him on the terrace, he was staring out at the ocean. Wrapping her arms around his waist, she asked, "You okay?"

He pulled her arms tighter. "Yep. For a vacation I didn't want, I'm not ready for it to be over."

She pressed her cheek to his back. "Yeah. I know what you mean."

They stood there for a minute, both of them lost in their own memories of the last nine days. Finally, Brock blew out a long breath. "I see the waiter on the beach setting up our breakfast. Ready?"

"Starved."

He laughed and pulled her around him until he could loop an arm over her shoulder. "We did burn up a few calories last night."

"And the night before that and the night before that," she said as they started walking toward the beach.

Brock loved to surprise her with breakfast. She never knew what he'd ordered until the cover was removed, but so far, he'd hit a home run every time. This morning was freshly-squeezed orange juice, more coffee (natch), Belgian waffles with fresh strawberries and whipped cream, and bacon. By the end of the meal, they'd decided to order a bowl of whipped cream with dinner, regardless of what dessert they ordered. In fact, Brock suggested only whipped cream for dessert, and she'd laughed.

The ride around the island was bittersweet. Natalie took her camera and shot pictures of everything, including Brock scowling when she aimed the camera at him, which only made her snap more.

That evening, dinner arrived as the sun was setting. The deep blue of the sky blended into purple, then pink, then orange at the water's edge.

"I wish I were a painter," Natalie said with a sigh. "Even my camera can't capture the beauty of the scene in front of me."

"I know what you mean," Brock said. "Beautiful."

She looked over to say something more about the setting sun and found Brock staring at her. Heat flushed her neck and up to her cheeks.

"I meant the sunset," she said.

"I didn't," he replied. "I meant you."

She cupped his cheek in her hand. "This week has been the best of my life."

He turned his head to place a kiss on her palm. "Mine, too."

Their final dinner together was a reprisal of their first...prime rib and key lime pie. The meat was tender and perfect, but Natalie could barely swallow around the lump that'd formed in her throat.

After dinner, after the sun had totally deserted them and the moon played hide-and-seek with the clouds, Brock pulled her onto the cushioned recliner on the terrace. She sat between his thighs, her back and head resting on his marble-like chest. He propped his chin on the top of her head, and they just sat there watching waves roll in.

Her mood was much like the waves...high one minute and crashing the next. Three or four times, she searched her brain for the right words to say, but she realized she didn't know what she wanted to tell Brock.

Thank you. You rocked my world.

Yeah, that seemed a little desperate.

But not as desperate as, *don't leave me*, and she'd had that thought, too.

Brock sighed a few times but seemed content to sit and hold her.

For some reason, the sitting and holding felt more intimate right now than if they'd been having wild monkey sex. Not that wild monkey sex would have been bad. Hell, no. That'd been awesome too, but this quiet time felt right. It felt as though both of them were soaking up the scents and feel of the other. Making memories to last a lifetime.

At ten, Brock kissed her neck. "It's getting late."

She shrugged. "I'm packed and ready. It won't take me long in the morning."

"Not what I meant. What I should have said was that I want to spend our last hours together naked and in bed."

A smile crawled across her mouth. "Yeah?"

"Yeah. And I'm pretty sure I'm ready to talk about the strings that were attached to this morning's coffee."

She twisted until her legs swung off the chair and

she was sitting sideways. She wrapped her hand around his neck and jerked him forward into a hot, deep, long kiss.

"Something like that?"

"I do love how you can read my mind."

Brock was up long before the five-a.m. alarm. He finished all his morning necessities before walking back into the bedroom to wake Natalie. For a few minutes, he just stood and watched her sleep. Her full lips puckered as she let out a little snore, which made him smile. If only she didn't snore, she'd be perfect.

Ah, hell. Who was he kidding? She was perfect. Perfect for him.

Yes, he realized they'd only known each other for less than two weeks, but his mother had always told him that when it was right, he would know.

He knew. This was right. She was the one for him, but how did tell her that without sending her fleeing from a lovesick cowboy? Would she hit the road running if he started blurting out professions of love after such a short period?

He wasn't exactly sure how Natalie felt about him. They hadn't discussed feelings. Besides, wasn't it the woman who was supposed to be the touchy-feely one? Shouldn't she be all emotional about leaving him? If she was, she sure hid it well.

"Stop staring at me," she growled and rolled over.

"And good morning to you, too," he said brightly.

"Bite me. Wake me when breakfast gets here. You wore me out last night."

"No breakfast this morning, Natalie. Remember?"

Her movements stopped abruptly at his words. "Right. Going home today. What time is it?"

"Almost five. You've got about ninety minutes, but we have to load our luggage, return the cars, check out, and get to the airport by then. I'm done in the bathroom if you want it."

She threw the covers back, the sight of her naked body sending him from semi-hard to painfully rigid in two breaths.

"Fine. Fine. I'm up," she said.

When she stretched her arms over her head, he had to fight the impulse to tackle her back onto the mattress and screwed her until she promised to come to Texas with him. But then she stood and walked past him, giving him a slap on his ass on her way to the bathroom.

He grinned. His gal was sassy, that's for sure. His family would love her.

The time flew and, before he realized it, they were climbing the stairs to the airplane. Their seats weren't together, but he fixed that by convincing a woman to exchange seats so he could sit by Natalie on the flight to San Juan. He took her hand at take-off and held it through the short thirty-minute flight.

She put her head on his shoulder with sigh. He

struggled to find the right words...words that could express everything he was feeling, but the timing didn't feel right. If anything, a confession of love might feel rushed and fake. He wanted her to believe that he'd fallen totally for her in only nine days. He only got one chance at this and it had to count. Maybe on the plane to Memphis they could talk.

At the San Juan airport, he asked about upgrading to first class to sit with her. When he couldn't, she asked about joining him in coach. But the flight was full and exchanges and upgrades were not happening.

They found seats together in the boarding area to wait.

"Brock, I don't know if I'll see you once we get to Memphis. I just want to tell you that this time together has been..." She choked a little. Saying goodbye was going to be harder than she'd thought. "It's been wonderful."

"It doesn't have to end. Come home with me. I can get off in Memphis. We can drive to the ranch. It's only about nine hours or so. Or change your flight and fly to Dallas with me."

Her heart raced at his words, but she was too grounded in reality to allow her fantasy to grow. "Oh, Brock, that is so sweet, but it's Christmas Eve. Your family is expecting you, not you and a guest."

"They'd love to meet you. They'll love you. I'm

sure of it. I can call home when we get to Memphis and let them know."

She felt her resolve to not go faltering. "I don't know, Brock. Christmas is such a family holiday."

He took her hand. "I don't want you to be alone tonight and tomorrow. Nobody should be alone at Christmas."

Before she could answer, the gate crew started boarding. She stood when they called first class. Brock didn't release her hand.

"Think about it. I would love for you to come to Ace in The Hole. Nobody should be alone for Christmas, especially someone as wonderful as you. Promise me you'll think about it?"

She nodded and leaned forward to kiss him. She pulled her hand from his and walked down the gateway to the plane.

By the time Brock's seat number was called, the plane was crowded, people shoving boxes and sacks into every free inch of space they could find. He gave her a wink as he passed. Her heart leaped, then fell deep into her belly. Her breath hiccupped as she fought tears.

"You look like you could use a drink," a pretty flight attendant said. "What can I get you?"

She started to say bourbon, but she knew she'd never drink bourbon again without thinking of him.

"Mimosa, please."

Shortly, a carton of orange juice and a small split of champagne appeared on her tray. "Let me know if you need anything else," the attendant said and walked on to help another passenger.

Natalie fixed a strong mimosa—a glass of champagne with two drops of orange juice—and drank to her incredible, unforgettable vacation.

During the flight, she replayed their time together at the Sand Castle...all the meals, the runs, the laughs, the loving. She stored each memory into its own special place in her mind.

Then, she replayed their gate conversation, and gasped as a realization hit like a pole axe between her eyes. He'd flat out told her he wanted her to come home with him because he didn't want her to be alone at Christmas. He'd felt sorry for her. That explanation made all the sense in the world.

She wanted to slap her forehead in frustration. That's why he'd asked her to come to his house.

She was such an idiot. She might have fallen for him like a ton of bricks, but he was a guy on vacation looking for a fun time, and she'd given him that. No promises had been made, except the one to herself to have fun. She was completely alone on her love boat.

He was a great guy, a man beyond any of her simple fantasies. But they lived in different states with a entire state sitting between them. She had to get it through her thick skull that this was the vacation fling she'd promised herself. She'd done it, and now it was time to go back to her world, her life.

Once she arrived in Memphis, the smart thing to do would be to get off the plane, grab her luggage from luggage claim, and wish him a nice life. Be mature about the whole sleeping together thing. They were adults. They'd had consensual sex. Okay, maybe consensual wild monkey sex, but it'd been sex, not a life-long commitment. No promises to see each other again. No emotional expressions of love. Nothing she could grab and hold on to.

In Memphis, she was first off the plane and didn't wait for him. She hurried down to luggage claim and prayed her luggage would get loaded on the carousel first.

Of course, it didn't. She was still standing there, waiting for the red light to blink and the conveyor belt to move, when she saw Brock striding toward her. His face looked tight, angry.

"You didn't wait for me," was his opening line.

"Was I supposed to?" Stupid response, but even though her heart was pounding gallons of blood through her body at a rapid rate, none of it seemed to be reaching her brain.

"What's going on, Natalie?" He took her arm and pulled her off to the side. "Talk to me."

She glanced nervously at the carousel, which remained frozen and quiet, then she looked at him.

"Nothing is going on, Brock. I'm home. You're headed home. We had a great time on vacation. Maybe it's best if we leave with our good memories intact."

His forehead pulled into a severe frown. "What in the hell are you talking about?"

"I can't come home with you. I thank you from the bottom of my heart for inviting me. For not wanting me to be alone tonight and tomorrow. But I'll be fine." She touched his cheek. "Really." She kissed him. "Thank you for caring."

"Damn it, Natalie. It's more than caring about you being alone." He raked his fingers through his short hair. "I don't know what it is, but it's damn sure more than worried about you being alone on a holiday."

"Go home. See your family. Smile when you remember me and our time at the Sand Castle."

The red light on the luggage carousel began to blink, and a loud horn honked.

"That's us." She turned to walk away when he grabbed her arm to stop her.

"This is it? You're walking away from...from..."

"Our fling? Yes. I understood going in that this wasn't a forever thing." She forced a smile and hoped her lips weren't quivering as hard as her knees. "Thank for you for making my vacation unforgettable." Her voice cracked ever so slightly. It was time to leave before she said or did something she'd regret in the morning. It was impossible to fall in love in only ten days. A little distance and she'd get her perspective back. She dug in her purse and pulled out a business card. "Call me sometime. Let me know you're okay."

He took her card and stared at it like he couldn't believe it was real, then shoved it in his front pocket. "Natalie..."

She bussed his cheek. "Goodbye, Brock."

She pulled out of his grasp and found her luggage

CYNTHIA D'ALBA

circling. She pulled it off, jerked up the handle and rolled it to her car. She didn't let herself cry until she was safely behind her wheel and pulling onto Winchester Road. And then the first large tear rolled down her cheek. It was followed by a gush of tears until she finally pulled to the side of the road. She laid her head on her steering wheel and cried.

Ten

Brock couldn't believe Natalie had walked away from him in Memphis. He'd been shocked when he'd gotten off the plane and she'd already headed to luggage claim. But when she'd told him goodbye in that cold emotionless voice, the jab to his gut had left him breathless.

The short flight from Memphis to Dallas didn't give him enough time to sort through all his thoughts and feelings. The traffic from Dallas to the ranch was thick with last-minute shoppers and crazy drivers. Brock swerved from hitting the back end of quite a few cars during his commute. By the time he pulled into the ranch drive, he'd pretty much used up his yearly allotment of cuss words.

But Natalie's walking away wasn't his only surprise of the day. The family home was decked out in twinkling lights from the roof to the eaves, to every pole on the porch. In the big picture window stood an enormous evergreen with sparkling lights, ornaments he hadn't seen in years, and old-fashioned tinsel. Wrapped packages were piled high under the tree.

He was home. A wave of pride swelled in his chest. His home. His ranch. He'd done this. He'd kept the ranch from going to creditors. He'd raised his younger siblings when he'd barely been old enough to vote. If only Natalie could see all this, maybe she'd understand that he knew what love and responsibility were. And when he said he loved her, he fully comprehended the meaning of those words. He vowed to call her tonight.

He was barely in the door when Hurricane Lauren whirled up and fired twenty questions at him, not giving him a chance to answer even the first one.

"Did you have fun? What was the resort like? Was it as great as it looked on the internet? Were there any movie stars there? I read that it was the *in* place for them. I saw the parasail pictures. Was it fun? Who was the girl in the picture with you? How were your flights?"

Laughing, he pulled his sister in and kissed her forehead. "It was great. The resort was incredible. No movie stars. Can I tell you more once I set my luggage down?"

George and Cody grinned up at him from the two living room sofas.

"Welcome home, bro," Cody said. "Guess what?"

"What?"

"We didn't burn down the house or barn while you were gone."

Brock laughed. "I knew you'd do fine."

And he had. Sort of. He just hadn't been willing to let go. As much as he hated to admit it, they had done fine without him for ten days. Maybe it was time to let them shoulder more of the responsibility around here. At least Cody and George should. Lauren was going to college. He'd sent Cody and George. He'd wanted to make sure they had more opportunities than he'd ever had.

Not that he begrudged his life. He didn't. He just hadn't realized how lonely it was until now.

Until Natalie.

"Okay then," he said, dropping his luggage at the foot of the stairs and coming back to the living room. He collapsed into his favorite chair with a sigh. "I know I gave you guys lots of crap about going, but thank you. The resort was more than I could've imagined. And okay, I'll admit it. I needed a vacation."

His two brothers high-fived each other. Brock shook his head but laughed.

"Pictures? You did bring me pictures, right?" Lauren was vibrating with barely contained energy.

"I have lots of pictures." He realized that Natalie would be in many of those photos, and he wasn't sure exactly how he would explain who she was. "So, tell me what I've missed."

Christmas morning brought frigid winds and stinging shards of sleet. The minute Brock's feet hit the cold hardwood floor, he longed for the hot days at the Sand Castle.

Holiday or not, there were cattle to feed and stalls to muck. At least the cows and horses didn't expect their chow today to come gift-wrapped.

As he worked, his mind was filled with images of Natalie. He'd meant to call her last night, but his siblings had wanted to hear every detail. The evening got away from him and before he'd known it, the hour had gotten late. This morning, he was debating if he should be trying to reach her or find a way to erase from his mind the sexiest, most unforgettable woman he had ever met. Surely ten hours of hard labor would help.

When he got downstairs, fresh coffee filled the pot. Biscuit and ham sandwiches were in the oven on warm. Dirty dishes sat in the sink. His siblings were nowhere to be seen.

After pouring a cup of coffee, he retrieved a hot biscuit sandwich from the oven. He leaned his hip on the counter as he ate, wondering where his siblings were. Wondering if, now that he was home, they'd slept in and handed all the responsibilities back to him.

He sighed. He knew it'd been too good to be true.

As he had the thought, the back door flew open and three icy humans stomped into the kitchen.

"Good lord it's cold out there," Lauren complained. She slapped her gloves together to knock off the ice before slipping them off and dropping them on the table. "Morning sleepyhead," she teased.

"You have perfect timing," George said. "We just finished feeding the horses. The barn can wait until this afternoon."

"What about the cattle?" Brock asked, still a little shocked that his siblings had handled most of the morning chores already.

"Hank and I will head out after breakfast and presents." Cody grinned. "We sort of have us a routine now. Hank and I take care of the stock. George and Lauren are in charge of the barn."

Brock nodded. "Sounds good. Who cooks and does the laundry?"

"Yeah, well. We were kind of hoping to talk you into a housekeeper."

Brock shook his head. "We can't afford it."

"Yeah, we can," Cody said. "I've been looking at the books and, ah, hell. This can wait until tomorrow. I say we get to the present opening."

Even as Brock followed his loud and boisterous family to the living room, he felt like a semi had driven through his chest, leaving a gaping hole. He plastered a smile on his face and joined them in the annual ripping into the Christmas presents.

After all the presents had been opened, and the givers thanked, Cody dragged George along to help with the cattle. He'd told Hank to stay home with his family and that George would take Hank's place. George had grumbled, but hadn't put up much of an argument.

The minute the door slammed in the kitchen, Lauren pounced on him. "You know, Brock, our brothers might have heads as thick as slabs of concrete, but I don't."

"I don't know what you're talking about." Brock picked up his empty coffee cup from the sofa table and stood to go to the kitchen.

"I saw the woman in all your pictures. Who is she?"

"Nobody," he lied, his heart breaking. How could she have just walked away like that?

"You are not the same Brock we sent on vacation."

He turned to face her with a glare. "I don't have any idea what you're rambling about." He whirled back and headed for the sink of dirty dishes.

She followed him.

"Lauren, just leave it be. Okay? I'm fine."

"You're not fine." He heard her sniff. "This is all my fault. I'm the one who pushed this vacation on you and everybody else."

"It's not your fault. I told you. I had a great vacation, so there's nobody at fault for anything. Aren't you supposed to go over to your friend's house for Christmas brunch?"

"That's not for another two hours."

He looked at her. She wasn't grown, but she wasn't a little girl anymore. But he damned sure wasn't discussing his love life with her...or any of his family.

"Look, pumpkin. The resort was incredible. The

weather was hot. The water was warm. The food was delicious. I'm just grumpy being back in cold, wet weather. That's all." He pasted on his plastic smile again. "Who'd want to leave paradise?"

"Are you sure that's all? Nothing else? *Nobody* else you want to talk about?"

"I'm sure. Nothing to talk about." He hugged her. "Now, get out of here and go on to the Pettys' house. I have laundry to do."

She hugged him back. "We're glad you're home."

"Me, too."

Once she left, the house fell into a deathly quiet. Brock slumped on the sofa. He'd screwed up. He didn't know how he'd screwed up, only that he had. What had he done or said to run Natalie off? The more he thought about it, the surer he was he hadn't done anything but fall hard for her. He was also sure that no matter what she said or did, Natalie felt as strongly about him as he did about her.

He hadn't gone looking for love but damned if it hadn't sneaked up and bit him on the ass.

Love. He'd fallen in love with Natalie Diamond. Even now, he could picture her standing at the sink in the kitchen, or snuggling up next to him on the sofa, or, better yet, naked and moaning in his bed. His cock woke up at that thought.

They owed it to each other to see where this relationship—or whatever it was—went. He had to know where she stood.

He pulled her card from his pocket and dialed her home phone number. The phone began to ring. The palms of his hands began to sweat. It was possible he was in this all by himself. It was possible that he had just been a fling for Natalie.

The phone rang until her message machine told him to leave a message.

"Merry Christmas, babe. This is Brock. Call me." He left his number.

After an hour when she hadn't called back, he rang her again. And again, he got her voice mail. Her business card hadn't had her private cell phone number, so her landline was the only connection unless he wanted to send an email, but what he had to say needed to be said, not typed into a computer.

Another hour passed and he got worried. What if something had happened on her drive home? If she'd been in an accident, nobody would know. Who knew to check whether she'd made it home safely last night? His family had been on the lookout for him, but her parents were on a cruise somewhere. He should have called her last night.

He heard the crunch of tires on the icy gravel. Probably one of Lauren's friends coming by to see her Christmas haul. He geared himself up for a giggling teenager and waited for the doorbell.

It took a while for Lauren's friend to make it from the car to the porch. By the time the doorbell rang, he was fully irritated at having to serve as his sister's doorman on Christmas.

He flung open the door and froze. A punch as solid as a mule kick hit him in the gut.

"Hi." Natalie stood looking up at him.

When he continued to stand there, she added, "Do you want me to leave?"

"No. Of course not. Come in."

He closed the door behind her. "I can't believe you're here."

"I'm here. And I'm freezing."

"Give me your coat. How did you get here?"

She slipped off the heavy winter coat and handed it to him. "I drove. You realize that between my house and your house is a lot of crappy weather, right? The simple seven-hour-drive you promised me took closer to ten."

He could feel her gaze on him as he hung her coat on a peg. His heart beat like a bass drum in his ears. His sweaty palms were back. He could hardly catch his breath.

"You came," he said.

"I came."

"Why?" He had to ask. He had to know if their feelings were the same.

"Why did you ask me to come? Was it because you didn't want me to be alone for Christmas?"

Their gazes met and held, each of them seemingly waiting on the other to speak first.

He took a step toward her. "I asked you to come because I knew what we had at the Sand Castle wasn't a vacation fling. At least, not for me. And I don't believe it was for you either."

She took a step closer to him. "It wasn't a fling."

"I..." He paused, knowing the next words would either send her into his arms or out his door. "I know it sounds impossible, but I've fallen in love with you."

She nodded. "I had the same thought. How can I be in love with a man I spent such a short time with, but I am. I love you, Brock."

When he smiled, she threw herself into his arms and covered his face with kisses. He caught her face between his hands and crushed her mouth in a deep kiss. They didn't need the words when their kisses spoke volumes.

I love you.

I love you too.

Don't go.

I'm not going anywhere.

Epilogue

F ive Months Later

"Are you sure you're okay with selling the house?" Natalie asked her mother.

"Without a doubt. I'll always have a special place in my heart for this place since I grew up here and raised you here, but honey, this house needs tons of work. A new furnace and new roof—just to name two of the things that have to be done—to speak nothing of the general updating. Besides, when your father and I moved to Florida, I knew I'd never come back to Memphis. After the time we've spent at our new place, I am more than sure we're never coming back." Sissy Diamond hugged her daughter. "So don't worry about it."

"Thanks, Mom. I think I just needed to hear you say you had no regrets."

"None. Besides, in this housing market, we sold it for more than we could ever dream, right, honey?" she said to her husband.

Charlie Diamond chuckled. "I'm thrilled."

Her mother and father exchanged glances, and then both of them laughed.

"Trust me," her mother said. "We are more than happy to have this albatross from around our necks."

"Mom!" Natalie admonished. "You guys did tell the new buyers all that's wrong with the house, didn't you?"

"Of course, we did," Sissy said. "Gerald and Bob have a bunch of plans to bring this house back to life."

Natalie's dad pulled her in for a hug and whispered in her ear. "Are you sure about moving to Texas? You can always come to Florida with us."

Natalie squeezed her dad. "More than sure, Dad." She stepped back and looked at her parents. "I'm sad about leaving Memphis, though. I mean, I've spent my whole life here."

Brock wrapped his arm around her shoulders. "You can always come back for visits with your friends."

She sighed. "I know, but it won't be the same." Then she looked up at her fiancé. "You're worth leaving home for."

"Aww. Thanks, babe." He brushed his lips over her temple.

"You're taking my baby," Charlie said. He pointed to his eyes and then toward Brock, indicating his eyes would be on Brock. "Take care of her."

"You don't have to worry about that, sir," Brock said. "She's my everything."

Sissy Diamond smiled. "Perfect answer."

"Honey, we need to get on the road," Brock said to Natalie.

"I know, I know." Natalie turned toward the house. "Let me walk through it one more time."

Brock smiled. "Sure, but hustle."

Natalie hurried up the brick steps and stepped between the brick and wood pillars onto the porch. Her favorite area—where the porch swing had hung —stood empty. The swing had been packed into the back of Brock's truck with her other belongings. She opened the red wooden door and walked into her empty living room. Her shoes tapped on the hardwood floors as she walked from empty room to empty room. No trace of her, or her family, remained anywhere. Every wall was blank, the need for fresh paint evident everywhere she looked.

In the kitchen, her ancient appliances waited to be turned on by the new owners. Through the window over the sink, she looked into her small backyard. The grass had been mowed, but no flowers bloomed this year. The area looked sad and lonely, something she was sure Gerald and Bob would fix.

With a smile, she walked back through the house and onto the porch. For a minute she watched her parents and the man she loved more than anything chatting beside his truck. Attached to the truck's trailer hitch was a flatbed car hauler with Natalie's SUV, packed front to back and top to bottom with clothes, shoes, and other items she felt were indispensable. All the furniture had been sold as her parents neither needed nor wanted anything they'd left behind with their move. When she, or rather Brock, pulled away today, she'd have left nothing of herself behind in Tennessee. New adventures awaited her in Texas, and she was ready to tackle the next stage of her life.

"Natalie!" Brock called. "We need to go."

"I'm coming, I'm coming," she said as she closed the door to the house and her Memphis life.

"Now, you drive safe," Sissy admonished. "Don't drive too fast."

"Yes, Ma'am," Brock replied.

Sissy tightly hugged her daughter before pulling Brock into an embrace. "I'm so happy to finally have a son," she told him with a smile.

"Can't wait to have you guys to the ranch," Brock told her.

"We're looking forward to it," Charlie said as he shook Brock's hand.

"I can't believe my baby is getting married in only two weeks," Sissy said with a sniff.

"Now, Sissy, don't start crying again," Charlie said.

Natalie's mom sniffed and wiped a couple of tears from her cheeks. "I'm not," she said. "Obviously, my allergies are acting up again."

Natalie laughed. "Sure, Mom." She bussed quick kisses on each of her parents' cheeks. "I'll pick you up at the Dallas airport in two weeks."

Brock opened the passenger door and held it as Natalie climbed up into his truck. He slammed the door and turned to her parents. "We'll see you soon, and don't worry." He tilted his head toward where Natalie sat. "I've got her."

As they pulled away from her childhood home, Natalie turned and waved to her parents standing in the drive. She watched them get smaller and smaller as the distance between the truck and house widened, until Brock turned to get onto I-40 heading toward Little Rock and then Texas.

She turned in her seat and looked at him.

"Having second thoughts?" he asked.

"No, but change is hard."

He reached over and took her hand. "I've got you," he said then pressed a kiss to her knuckles.

She settled back for the ride. She was safe and happy with him and could she ask for anything more?

Two Week Later

"Knock, knock."

Natalie looked up from her makeup mirror and toward the door of her bedroom. "Come in."

And yes, she and Brock had been staying in separate bedrooms. On the drive down, they'd decided not sleeping together during these two weeks could serve two purposes. The first was as a role model for Lauren, who was still at an impressionable age when it came to love. The second was a selfish one for them. Not spending the nights together would make their wedding night even more special than it already would be.

Lauren popped her head around the edge of the door. "Can I come in?

"Of course."

Lauren closed the door behind her and dropped onto Natalie's bed. "Your parents are here."

"Oh great. Thank you for picking them up at the airport."

"No problem. I like your mom."

Natalie chuckled. "Watch out. You'll find yourself adopted."

Lauren shrugged. "I like your mom. She seems pretty cool."

Natalie grew serious. "I know you've been without a mother for a long time, and there's no way I'll replace her, but I want you to know that Brock and I will always be here for you. And if not us, call my mom. Sissy Diamond would love to have another daughter."

Lauren smiled. "I might do that." She scooted across the bed until she was sitting on the edge closest to Natalie. "I have to tell you that I'm sorry."

Natalie frowned. "For what?"

"I wasn't the most supportive person when I found out about you and Brock."

Not supportive was a mild understatement. Lauren had been shocked when she'd returned home Christmas afternoon and walked in on Brock and Natalie in an intimate embrace. She'd told Brock that Natalie was after all their money and the ranch, which had made Brock break into laughter.

That night, he had sat Lauren, along with her

two brothers and Natalie, down for a long talk. He'd shown them the financials of the ranch, the income and the expenses. In all the years he'd been older brother and parent to these three, he'd tried to never let them know how close they'd skated to bankruptcy and losing everything. Yes, there had been some small life insurance policies that'd gone into effect when their parents had died, but nothing like the influx of cash that'd been needed.

Natalie hadn't been surprised. Brock had told her all of this while they'd been at the Sand Castle, so she was coming into the marriage with a full understanding of their financial situation. It didn't scare her in the least. Brock and she had some exciting plans for growing the ranch revenue, but that talk with the siblings would come when the time was right.

The three siblings had been stunned. The older ones, his two brothers, had been upset that he'd spent so much money on them going to college when they could have been here on the ranch. But Brock had waved off their gripes, unmoved by their protests. He'd explained to Natalie that if his brothers decided to stay on the ranch, it would be their decision based on their desires and not based on not having other options. He'd handed the keys to their lives with a college education. What they did with those keys were up to them.

When Lauren suggested she skip college, the three brothers had presented a united front, insisting she would go. Just like Brock had done for brothers, he wanted his sister to have all the tools and education to do something other than ranching, if that's what she desired. Natalie had agreed with this reasoning and the four adults presented a united front to Lauren. Later that night, Natalie had told Brock that Lauren had looked relieved that she wasn't going to have to forgo college, even if she had no idea what she was going to study.

"I'm sure discovering all the hardships that Brock had faced raising you three was a shock." Natalie said and then she grinned. "At least you knew I wasn't after all the money."

Lauren's cheeks pinkened. "Still, I was being a brat and I feel horrible about it. I see how happy Brock is since you've come into this life."

Natalie chuckled. "He makes me happy, too, Lauren, as does having you and your brothers in my life. I never had siblings, and I've grown to love you all so much."

"Thank you for asking me to be your maid of honor today."

Natalie moved to the bed and sat by the teenager. "You're the one I wanted by me."

"But your friends?'

Natalie put her arm around Lauren. "Are my friends, but you are my family."

Lauren sniffed. "Thank you."

"Help me get into my dress?"

"Sure, I promised your mom I'd come get her and the photographer before you got dressed. Shoot,

122

A COWBOY'S SEDUCTION

that's why I came in here to begin with. I was supposed to tell you the photographer is here."

Natalie chuckled. "Okay, maid of honor. Go get the pre-wedding troops and let's get this show on the road."

Lauren hurried from the room. Natalie looked into her mirror and smiled at herself. Everyone said brides had a special sparkle on their wedding day, and darn if she didn't have a bright twinkle in her eyes. Not only was she marrying the love of her life, she was finally getting Brock back in her bed.

After her visit with Brock at Christmas, she'd gone back to Memphis to give her notice at her job. However, being that it was the start of the crazy tax season, it wouldn't have been right to leave her company in a lurch.

Besides, she and Brock had decided to spend time getting to know each other better before taking this big step, but honestly, she'd known on Christmas day when he'd opened the door that she would never want to be with another man. Brock Wade was it for her.

Today was the day she'd been waiting five long months for.

Her mom burst through the door, a tall photographer and his assistant following behind her.

"I'm here," Sissy cried. "Let's get this wedding going."

At seven that evening, Natalie walked through a field of Texas Bluebells, down the white runner between rows of white chairs that'd been set up on Ace in the Hole ranch for this occasion. Dressed in a new black suit, black cowboy boots, and a new Stetson, Brock stood waiting for her. As she neared, she saw tears in his eyes. She placed her hand in his and stepped beside him.

"You are beautiful," he said.

"You are, too," she said.

"I love you," he said.

"I will always love you," she replied.

He squeezed her hand and they turned as one to face the wedding officiant, his brother Cody, who'd gotten licensed online so he could do this ceremony.

"Ladies and Gentlemen," Cody began. "We're here today to celebrate the best decision my brother has ever made, marrying this wonderful woman."

The small audience chuckled, as did Natalie and Brock.

Natalie smiled. She couldn't help thinking that this day and their love was destined to be. Living hundreds of miles apart in two different states, their lives might never have crossed if not for their families. Their families had given them bigger Christmas gifts than they ever could have imagined with their forced vacations.

They'd gifted them both with a lifetime of love.

Note From the Author

Thank you for reading A Cowboy's Seduction. I appreciate my readers. Without you, I wouldn't be here.

Readers are always asking: What can I do to help you?

My answer is always the same: PLEASE give me an honest review. Every review helps.

Read on for excerpts from other books in the Diamond Lakes, Texas series.

Stay in touch with my newsletters by going to https://cynthiadalba.com/newsletter-sign-up/

Cynthia

About the Author

About the Author:

New York Times and USA Today Bestselling author Cynthia D'Alba was born and raised in a small Arkansas town. After being gone for a number of years, she's thrilled to be making her home back in Arkansas living in a vine-covered cottage on the banks of an eight-thousand acre lake.

When she's not reading or writing or plotting, she's doorman for her spoiled border collie, cook, housekeeper and chief bottle washer for her husband and slave to a noisy, messy parrot. She loves to chat online with friends and fans.

You can find her most days at one of the following online homes:

Website: cynthiadalba.com

Facebook:Facebook/cynthiadalba

Twitter:@cynthiadalba

Newsletter: https://cynthiadalba.com/news letter-sign-up/

She loves to hear from her fans and readers!

Drop her a line at cynthia@cynthiadalba.com
Or send snail mail to: Cynthia D'Alba PO Box
2116 Hot Springs, AR 71914

Read on for excerpts from
Diamond Lakes, Texas books
by
Cynthia D'Alba

Texas Justice

DIAMOND LAKES, TEXAS BOOK 1

A first-term Sheriff is torn between duty and love when the Chief of Surgery is accused of medical malpractice and homicide.

Following an auto accident and a death during surgery, Sheriff Kyle Monroe is pulled between professional responsibilities and his personal life. He's ready to stand by Dr. Tess Sweeney to fight bogus medical malpractice charges, even under pressure from his doctor brother and the county District Attorney distance himself from her. He has to clear her of the charges to keep their new found love going.

Read on for an excerpt:

"Sorry, ma'am. I'm gonna have to frisk you."

"But, Sheriff, I didn't do anything," Tess Sweeney said, rapidly batting her eyelashes. "I swear."

She dragged out the last two words in the best damned Scarlet O'Hara imitation she could do. The corners of his mouth twitched for a minute before his face transformed into a stern expression.

"Spread 'em," he ordered, deepening his voice into a growl.

"If I don't, are you going to pistol whip me?" She made a point of sticking out her lower lip in a pout.

"No, ma'am, but I might have to use my big nightstick on you."

Tess squealed with laughter. "Has that line ever worked?"

Tess looked up into the steel-gray eyes of Kyle Monroe. He gave her a smile that sent her heart racing. Sexual energy flared, melting her insides.

"Nope, but a man's gotta have hope." He brushed the back of his fingers along her cheek. She pressed her face into his touch. His eyes darkened with desire. Every cell in her body lit up.

"Have I told you how beautiful you are?"

A huge lump formed in her throat. Too thin and too plain as a child, she'd never had much attention from boys. By the time she'd reached high school, she'd developed large breasts, a narrow waist, and hips that swung when she walked. But inside, she was still that skinny, ugly little girl nobody picked for their kickball team.

Tess's elbows sank into the mattress as she arched her back, crushing her breasts against his chest. She savored the feel of the rough hair there against her sensitive nipples. "You might have mentioned it once or twice over dinner." She ran her tongue around his nipple and caught it between her teeth, tugging gently on the rigid flesh.

He caught her head between his hands, holding her against his chest. His deep-throated moan told her how much he loved the rasp of her tongue on his flesh.

Moving up his body, she kissed and nibbled until she reached his lower lip. She sucked it between her lips and then looked at him. "But for now, less talk. More action." She raked her taut nipples through his chest hair again.

"Yes, ma'am," he said as he rolled her onto her back and worked his way down her neck.

Beside her right ear her cell phone vibrated on the oak bedside table. It pulsated twice more, followed by loud gonging.

"Argh," she moaned, dropping her arms out to her sides. Did she have to get a call the first time she was in bed with this incredibly sexy man? Of course she did.

"Don't answer it," he said, tightening his arms around her like a steel band.

"You know I have to." She glanced at the clock and sighed. One a.m. Nobody got good news at this hour. "I'm on call. No choice."

Cadillac Cowboy

DIAMOND LAKES, TEXAS BOOK 3

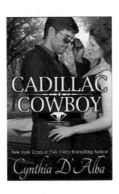

From NYT-USA Today Best Selling Author comes a story of a cop, an antique Cadillac, and a bride on the run from her mob fiancé. What could possibly go wrong?

Relocating from Chicago to Texas, cop Shade Gruber agrees to drive his grandmother's prize car to his new home in Diamond Lakes. He expects some car issues. He doesn't expect to pick up a runaway bride.

Bride Victoria Vaught dashes from the church thirty minutes before the *I Do*s. Stranded in her bridal attire when her car breaks down, she starts walking, desperate to get as far from Chicago as possible.

Their road to love is filled with twists, turns and bumps...and a stolen flogger! Hanging on to the one you love can be a roller coaster ride with surprising results.

Read on for an excerpt:

Despite the moniker hung on him by his parents, Shade Gruber had never had trouble picking up women. Tall. Short. Blonde. Brunette. Thin. Not so thin. Didn't matter to him. He loved them all.

However, in all his thirty-four years, he'd never picked up a woman walking down the road in a wedding dress. And not just any wedding dress. The bell-shaped skirt took up about one-third of his lane, the once-white hem now black from dragging along the pavement. A long train of veil flowed down from the tiara on the bride's head to the skirt's hem.

His mind flashed to the late model Jaguar on the side of the road he'd passed a couple of miles back.

He pulled alongside the bride. His eyebrows lifted in surprise. Of all the runaway brides in the world..."Howdy. Need some help?"

She stopped walking and glanced toward him. "Why would you think a woman walking on a country highway in a horrific wedding dress while wearing Spanx and high heel shoes would need help?" She blew out a puff of air that lifted her wilted bangs off her forehead.

Spanx? He couldn't imagine what that was.

"Well, okay then," he said. "Have a nice evening." He let his vintage Cadillac convertible roll forward about a hundred feet to give her time to change her mind.

"Wait."

And bingo.

She hiked up the front of the dress and jogged to the passenger side, her heels clacking on the road's pavement. Panting, she blew her hair off her forehead again. With the convertible top and windows down, Shade had been enjoying his drive in the cool, fall evening air. Now, all that openness allowed the renegade bride to pop the lock on the passenger side, open the door, and climb into the rear seat, scraping stiff lace over his head in the process. As his hitchhiker positioned herself in the middle of the seat, the massive volume of tulle and satin spread out around her.

"Oops." She leaned forward until she could get a hand on the open door and closed it with a slam. Then she settled back with a sigh.

Shade put the car in drive and pulled back onto the highway. "Where you headed? That your car on the side of the road back there?"

"Where am I headed?" she repeated. "Let's just say...*not* Chicago."

He nodded. "That's probably good since you were walking south."

"Where you headed?"

"Texas."

"Texas. Never been there. Texas," she said again, as though rolling the idea around in her mind. "Yeah. That works." Her dress rustled as she scooted to the edge of her seat and rested her arms on the backs of the front seats. "Why are you going to Texas?"

"New job." He glanced over at her and back to the road. "Why are you?"

"Like I said, it's not Chicago."

"So, did you cut out before the vows or after?"

Hot SEAL, Cold Beer

DIAMOND LAKES, TEXAS BOOK 2

An ex-Navy SEAL agrees to play fake lover for the Maid of Honor at a destination wedding only to discover that what happens on a Caribbean Island can sometimes follow you home.

Nicholas Falcone, aka Nikko, aka Falcon, is five months out from active SEAL duty, putting his pre-service accounting degree to use while going to law school at night. He'd love to take a vacation between semesters, but every buck is earmarked for his education. When a fellow accountant approaches him about his sister needing an escort for a destination wedding, Nikko jumps at the idea. With the wedding families footing the bill, what does he have to lose?

Surgeon Dr. Jennifer Pierce is still stinging from a broken engagement. Going to a destination wedding at the Sand Castle Resort in the Caribbean would be great if only her ex-fiancé and his new wife weren't also attending. Her options are to find a date or not go, but not going isn't really an option. That means letting her brother set her up with a guy from his accounting office...Heaven forbid. When did accountants start looking like this?

** Cold Beer ** is part of the Diamond Lakes, Texas Series and Sand Castle Resort series. Each book can be read as a stand-alone. They do not have cliffhanger endings.

Hot SEAL, Cold Beer is also in the "SEALs in Paradise" connected series. Each book in the multi-author branded SEALs in Paradise series can be read stand-alone, and individual books do not have to be read in any particular order.

Read on for an excerpt:

If there was one thing Dr. Jennifer Pierce hated, it was not being in control. She'd rather tell people what to do than be told. She despised surprises and was much more comfortable in situations where she had all the information. And, most importantly, she maintained a firm discipline over all emotions, especially her own.

However, right now, she was as nervous as a first-year med student holding a scalpel in surgery, and that irritated her, which only amped up her anxiety.

She agitated the martini shaker violently, the ice clanging against the stainless-steel container like a hail storm. After pouring the dry martini into a glass, she took a long, steadying sip.

Yeah, that didn't help her nerves.

On the other hand, the stiff drink didn't hurt, either.

With a resigned sigh, she walked to the living room and sat to await Nicholas Falcone. Her brother, Robert, had suggested Falcone as her potential date for a fast-approaching destination wedding. She loved her twin brother and trusted him...mostly. Because historically, the men he believed perfect for her had been so far off the mark as to be not even in the same book, much less on the same page. But she was between a rock and a slab of granite.

All she knew about this Falcone guy was he worked at McKenzie, Gladwell and Associates with her brother and had been a Navy SEAL. Weren't they called jarheads? Hell, she didn't know. She took another gulp of the cold vodka. What she knew about the military wouldn't fill a shot glass.

She'd give her brother credit for one thing. If Falcone's online photo was anywhere accurate, Nicholas Falcone looked the part she needed him to play. When Robert had called her to tell her about his solution to her dateless dilemma, she'd pulled up her brother's accounting firm on the internet to look at the staff photos and had been pleasantly surprised.

The picture had been of a gorgeous guy with a neatly trimmed beard, a sexy smile, and mischievous eyes. Man, she hoped he could carry on a decent conversation and not grunt answers to everything.

Her doorbell pealed, and her heart jumped in response. Pressing her hand over her quaking stomach, she drew in a calming breath, not that a calming breath had ever helped. So she took the next best option to deep breathing and finished off her martini.

Carrying her empty glass with her, she opened the door and looked at her potential blind date. Her brain hiccuped or maybe quit functioning altogether. He didn't look at all like she'd expected and prepared for. In person, he was...more. A whole lot more. With his chiseled cheeks and sharp chin, he was a million times more attractive in real life. His green eyes—a billion times more beautiful than that black-and-white photo showed—held an amused twinkle that coordinated handsomely with his amused smile. And his body? Dear lord. Broad shoulders pulled a white, oxford shirt tightly across them. Long sleeves rolled to mid-forearm exposed thick, ropey muscles that bunched and flexed when he extended his hand.

"Dr. Pierce. I'm Nikko Falcone."

She stepped back, embarrassed that she'd been staring at him. "Of course. I'm sorry. I was...never mind. Not important. Come in."

He lowered his hand and stepped into her foyer. The roomy area shrank. She'd expected tall and well-built, but the degree of just how brawny he was registered with a clunk upside her head.

Taking a step back, she gestured with her martini glass. "I'm having a drink. Can I fix you something?"

"A cold beer, if you have one."

"Sure. Have a seat." She flipped her hand toward the living room.

Beer in her refrigerator wasn't the norm. She wasn't much of a beer drinker, but since she hadn't known much about Nicholas Falcone's drink preferences—or anything at all about him really—she'd stocked a six-pack of beer as well as red wine, white wine, and the makings for any mixed drink imaginable. Always prepared, was her motto.

She would have made a hell of a boy scout.

She pulled out a cold bottle, cracked off the top, and got a chilled beer stein from her freezer. While she was there, she also poured herself a fresh vodka martini. Realizing she had too many items and not enough hands, she loaded everything on a tray and went back to the living room.

"I brought you a glass," she said, setting the tray on the glass coffee table in front of him. She lifted her martini and took the chair across from him.

"Bottle's fine," he said and took a long draw off the bottle.

She hid her discomfort with his drinking beer straight from the bottle. The people at the destination wedding they would be attending ran in high-society circles. Beer from bottles had been fine back in college, but now that they were all in their thirties, she was sure her friends, like her, had progressed to more sophisticated drinks and glasses.

Mentally, she made a note to talk with him about appearances.

He leaned back on her white sofa, stretched his arm across the back, and crossed an ankle over his knee. That's when she saw a tattoo peeking out from where the sleeve of his white oxford had been rolled up. From this distance, she could make out tines. A trident? As a doctor, she knew all about the infections that went with tattoos, and she wanted to disapprove. Instead, she got a little turned on. She didn't like that, or she shouldn't like that.

Damn. He had her all confused.

"So," she said, trying to gather her wits and the reins to the conversation. "What did Robert tell you?"

"In a nutshell, you had a fiancé. A big-time corporate lawyer. Said legal-eagle dirtbag got his secretary pregnant. Married her. Dumped you when he got back from his honeymoon. That about right?"

She winced. "In a nutshell."

He lifted the bottle to his lips—which she couldn't help notice were full and soft. Of course she noticed. She was a doctor. She always observed the human body...especially one like this.

He swallowed. His Adam's apple rose and fell with the action.

She had to get her air conditioning fixed. This room was too warm.

Also by Cynthia D'Alba

Snowy Montana Nights

Carmichael Triplets Trilogy (coming soon)

Hot Assets

Hot Ex

Hot Briefs

SEALs in Paradise

Hot SEAL, Alaskan Nights

Hot SEAL, Confirmed Bachelor

Hot SEAL, Secret Service (novella)

Hot SEAL, Sweet & Spicy

Hot SEAL, Labor Day

Hot SEAL, Girl Crush (coming Aug. 2022)

Mason Security

Her Bodyguard

His Bodyguard

Made in the USA
Columbia, SC
29 June 2022

62247706R10085